Their gazes seemed to lock and hold.

It was kissing that was on Neily's mind.

Kissing was on Wyatt's mind, too—she knew it as surely as if she were reading words on a page.

This might not have qualified as a date, but it still *felt* like one. Like a really great date. The kind of date where two people hit it off.

And *had* this been a really great date, a kiss good night now would have been the natural course of events.

Which might have been why she discovered herself leaning ever-so-slightly forward, her chin tipped ever-so-slightly upward.

Which might also have been why he seemed to be inching ever-so-slightly toward her…

Before he stopped.

To her relief.

And dismay.

Dear Reader,

We're back home in Northbridge and looking in on Neily Pratt. As the local social worker, Neily is investigating the latest turn of events—elderly and confused Theresa Hobbs Grayson took her caregiver's car keys and somehow managed to get from her current home in Missoula to the small town where she grew up long ago. Neily must determine if Theresa is getting the care she needs.

One of the three guardians Neily has to evaluate is Theresa's grandson, Wyatt Grayson. This proves more complicated than other cases Neily has handled because one look at Wyatt makes Neily's head go light.

Wyatt has nearly the same response to Neily, but a tragedy in his own recent past has left him hesitant to jump into another relationship. So while Neily is trying desperately to maintain her professionalism, Wyatt is trying just as desperately to keep control over his attraction to Neily. But that attraction is awfully strong. Maybe stronger than either of them…

I hope you're as glad to be back in Northbridge again as I am!

Always wishing you the best,

Victoria Pade

HOMETOWN SWEETHEART

VICTORIA PADE

Silhouette

SPECIAL EDITION®

Published by Silhouette Books

America's Publisher of Contemporary Romance

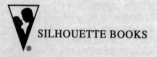

SILHOUETTE BOOKS

ISBN-13: 978-0-373-24929-9
ISBN-10:   0-373-24929-2

HOMETOWN SWEETHEART

Copyright © 2008 by Victoria Pade

Visit Silhouette Books at www.eHarlequin.com

Printed in U.S.A.

Books by Victoria Pade

VICTORIA PADE

is a native of Colorado, where she continues to live and work. Her passion—besides writing—is chocolate, which she indulges in frequently and in every form. She loves romance novels and romantic movies—the more lighthearted the better—but she likes a good, juicy mystery now and then, too.

Chapter One

"You said you had a plunger and you knew how to use it—I just took you up on it." Neily Pratt teased Charlie, the plumber she'd known for as long as she could remember. Charlie was only one of many townsfolk in Northbridge, Montana, who had just spent their entire Sunday working on the run-down old Hobbs house, a brick mammoth at the top of the hill at one end of South Street in the heart of Northbridge proper.

The house had been deserted until a week ago when its longtime owner, Theresa Hobbs Grayson, had somehow managed to steal the car of the live-in nurse who cared for her and make her way from her current residence in Missoula to her former hometown. Once she'd reached Northbridge, she'd abandoned the car at the ice cream parlor, walked the remaining block and a half to the house and slipped in through the cellar door.

Suffering from mental illness, Theresa had spent a few days undetected before she was discovered. When local police had entered the premises, she'd run for an upstairs bedroom, locking herself in. In her disturbed state of mind, she had hysterically refused to leave either the bedroom or the residence itself, saying that she was there to get back what was taken from her. The police had been forced to call in Human Services. Which, in Northbridge, meant sole social worker Neily Pratt, who was now overseeing Theresa's welfare and, for the time being, staying with Theresa at the old Hobbs house.

Neily's brother Cam joined her on the front porch where she was saying thanks and good-night to everyone as they left.

"Are you doing okay here alone?" Cam asked as he stood beside Neily and waved to someone heading off down the hill. Cam was one of the local police officers, and he, too, had done what he could today to make the house more livable.

"I'm fine," Neily assured her brother, knowing he was concerned for her safety. In her line of work Neily had encountered people who could be a danger to her, but she didn't believe the sweet seventy-five-year-old woman was one of them.

"Have there been any more scenes like the night we found her?" Cam persisted.

"The only time Theresa gets really difficult is when I say anything about her leaving the house. As long as I don't mention that, she's a lamb. So for now it seems better for her and easier for everyone else if she stays here while we figure out a long-term plan."

"Well, at least the place is cleaner and there aren't any more fire hazards. And the kitchen sink is unclogged and all the broken windows have been replaced," Cam observed.

"Thanks to you and our local Good Samaritans banding together to help me today. I especially appreciate the windows—we may be having a warm April but it still gets cold at night, and cardboard taped over gaping holes isn't a lot of help."

Neily and Cam exchanged a few final words with the electrician who came outside at that moment. Then the man went to his van parked in the driveway.

"Anyhow," Neily continued, "I haven't seen even a hint that Theresa is violent. Her mood is up and down, she's confused more than not, but she isn't a threat to anyone. I'll never understand how she made it here on her own—she must have been really determined. But now she mostly just sits silently in the rocking chair in the master bedroom."

"Like she has all day today—I never saw her."

"No one did. She didn't want to see anyone. But I didn't want her alone in the bedroom the whole day either—"

"So you hired a companion."

"Only after I promised Theresa that it wouldn't be

anyone who had known her in the past. I have no idea why that was such a big deal, but it was."

Out came three more volunteers—including sixteen-year-old Missy Hart, Theresa's companion—and after another round of gratitude and good-nights, Cam said, "Theresa's okay inside alone?"

"She'll still be sitting in the rocking chair when I go up to her—that's why I told Missy she could leave. I have a hard time getting Theresa to even come out of the bedroom, and since she's been in a panic at the thought of seeing anyone she used to know, she won't come out for sure until I let her know the coast is clear."

"Any early opinions on our geriatric runaway?"

Neily didn't consider it a breach of confidentiality to tell her brother what she knew because Cam had already been involved with the case.

"Theresa's physical exam showed no indications of mistreatment—and she isn't claiming any when I can get her to answer my questions. She's well fed, well dressed, clean. All in all, she's sound of body, if not of mind. The caseworker in Missoula has done some preliminary checking of the caregiver and the grandson who are coming sometime soon. So far they've been cleared to take over again temporarily when they get here. Under my supervision, anyway. The rest will take interviews and assessment—I'll do that here with Theresa and with whoever comes to be with her."

"But mentally, Theresa is really…off," Cam said kindly.

"She has a lot of issues, yes. Memory for one—she

keeps forgetting who I am and calling me Mikayla. When I ask who Mikayla is, she can't—or won't—tell me. She does seem to like Mikayla, though."

Against the tide of cars, trucks, vans and people on foot streaming down the hill, an SUV Neily didn't recognize made slow progress toward the house.

"If *that's* another reporter coming here, *I* might get violent," she told her brother with a nod at the approaching vehicle.

There had been a public search for Theresa in Missoula. Once she was located in Northbridge, reporters had begun descending on the small town in search of a follow-up story, and they'd become a nuisance.

"I'll check it out and get rid of them," Cam offered. Then, with a glance at Neily as he headed down the porch steps, he said, "You should wash your face—it's full of fireplace soot."

The last group of volunteers came out of the house right then, though, and Neily remained on the porch to say good-night to them, merely brushing blindly at her face in hopes of cleaning it as much as possible.

By the time that last group had left, Cam was back— with guests who seemed shocked by their first glimpse of the house.

"Not a reporter," Cam informed her as the man and a heavyset woman followed him onto the porch. "This is Theresa's grandson, Wyatt Grayson, and her caregiver, Mary Pat Gordman."

Wonderful. And I'm a mess, Neily thought.

She'd known even before her brother's earlier

comment that her clothes were soiled and her shoulder-length, chocolate-colored hair was falling shaggily from her ponytail. It certainly wasn't how she normally presented herself professionally. And if that wasn't bad enough, one glimpse of Theresa's grandson only made Neily more self-conscious because she guessed him to be her own age—and he was eye-poppingly handsome.

Not that it mattered under the circumstances, but it definitely didn't make Neily happier to be unkempt herself. It made her feel at a disadvantage.

There wasn't a thing she could do about it, though, so she pretended nothing was amiss and in her most professional-yet-friendly tone of voice, she said, "Hi, I'm Neily Pratt, Theresa's caseworker."

The caregiver hung back but Wyatt Grayson stepped up to meet Neily, standing tall, confident, broad-shouldered, and just muscular enough for the khaki slacks and navy-blue sports shirt he was wearing to give evidence to the fact that he probably worked out.

And then he took a real look at Neily and did a double take.

Do I look that bad?

"I'm sorry about—" she waved her hand up and down in front of herself "—this. We've been cleaning decades of dirt today."

Wyatt Grayson shook his head as if he were dumb-struck. "No, it isn't that," he muttered. Then the dark-blond eyebrows that matched his hair rose from a *V* into twin arches and he said, "You just look something like—"

"Someone named Mikayla?" Neily guessed. "Because Theresa keeps calling me that."

"Mikayla," Wyatt Grayson repeated, his deep baritone voice echoing with something Neily couldn't pinpoint. "Yes. Mikayla."

No wonder Theresa kept getting confused then.

But Wyatt Grayson didn't explain who Mikayla was, leaving Neily still curious as he recovered himself and held out a hand for her to shake. "Good to meet you, Miss Pratt."

"Neily," she amended.

She didn't know why, but she was uncommonly eager to accept that handshake. And once she had, she was also far too aware of every detail, every nuance of the meeting of his skin with hers, of the feel of that hand closing around hers—big, warm, strong, adept...

It was one of the oddest things she'd ever experienced.

But noticing all she was noticing about that simple handshake—and liking it—had no place in this so she ended the contact in a hurry.

Cam spoke up then, while Wyatt Grayson continued to study Neily with intense pewter-gray eyes.

"I have to get to the station, Neily," Cam said. "My shift starts soon. Unless you need me..."

"No, go ahead," Neily answered her brother, despite the fact that Wyatt Grayson's scrutiny was beginning to make her uncomfortable. She was grateful when he turned to say goodbye to Cam.

But given the opportunity to do some scrutinizing of

her own when Wyatt Grayson wasn't looking, Neily couldn't seem to stop herself.

His gleaming, sun-streaked dark-blond hair was cut short on the sides and slightly longer on top where he wore it in a natural disarray that gave him a casual, devil-may-care look. He had a perfectly shaped, straight nose. His lips were a little on the thin side but had a sort of sexy quirk to their corners. The bone structure of that photogenic face was a sharply defined collection of angles and hollows composed of high cheekbones, lean cheeks and a sculpted jawline. Plus there were those eyes! Sultry gray that she'd already seen reflect silver one minute and blue the next.

But none of that was a factor in anything, she reminded herself. He could have male-model good looks—and, actually, he did—but it wouldn't—couldn't—affect her assessment of him as one of his grandmother's guardians.

"Why don't we go inside?" Neily suggested after her brother headed for his car.

"How is my grandmother? Is she okay? The social worker in Missoula said she was no worse for wear, but her mental state is fragile and she isn't exactly young. Even so, this was an amazing thing for her to do—my brother, sister and I still can't believe she did it."

Neily judged it a positive sign that he was so concerned for Theresa. She led him and the caregiver into the house.

"The Missoula caseworker didn't mislead you. Theresa is okay as far as I can tell—not knowing anything about how she was before this," Neily said. "'None the worse for wear' is probably accurate."

"I want to apologize for no one in the family getting here immediately when authorities reached me on Thursday," Wyatt Grayson said as Neily closed the door behind them. "My sister was in Mexico dealing with a fire in a factory we have down there. She hated leaving at a time like this, but it was an emergency situation and we needed someone there. My brother was with the police in Canada—someone had read about Gram's disappearance and thought he'd try to cash in on it by calling in a ransom demand, and we had to take it seriously. I was alone in Missoula with all the commotion of the search there. Once I was told where Gram was, it seemed like Human Services bogged down Mary Pat and me with so many questions and so much red tape that it was as if they were purposely tying us up in Missoula to keep us from rushing down here. It's been a nightmare."

"I'm sure," Neily said.

She didn't tell him that he was right, that the caseworker in Missoula *had* purposely delayed him until it seemed relatively clear that harm wasn't likely to come to Theresa through contact with either him or with Theresa's nurse. "Once the police realized that your grandmother was here, I was brought in and I've been looking after her ever since, so there wasn't any hurry."

"Still, I wouldn't want you to get the wrong impression—we've all been crazy-worried about Gram and would have been here in a heartbeat if we could have."

Neily led the two new arrivals from the entry into the living room.

"Where is Gram?" Wyatt Grayson asked, glancing around in search of his grandmother.

"Why don't you and Ms. Gordman—"

"Mary Pat," the larger woman said, her first words.

"Why don't you and Mary Pat have a seat and I'll try to get Theresa down here to see you? She's been in the bedroom all day and I'd like her to come out if she's willing," Neily told them.

Neither the nurse nor the grandson accepted the invitation to sit, and Neily's impression was that they were both too concerned about Theresa to relax. That, too, seemed like a good indication they truly cared for the woman.

Neily excused herself and retraced her steps to the entryway, climbing the stairs to the second level.

She knocked lightly on the door of the master suite but didn't wait for a response from inside. She'd already learned that more often than not Theresa was too lost in her own world to even hear the knock.

Neily had predicted that Theresa would be sitting in the rocking chair and that was exactly where the older woman was, rocking back and forth as if the motion soothed her, staring at nothing in particular.

Theresa Hobbs Grayson was a relatively small woman—a full four inches shorter than Neily's five-foot-four-inch height. But she was somewhat rounder than Neily, who didn't carry many extra pounds. Theresa's salt-and-pepper-hued hair was cut short and neat, and while her gray eyes didn't hold the luster and life and different play of colors that her grandson's did, it struck

Neily that Wyatt had inherited his own sparkling gray eyes from his grandmother. Along with his good looks, because Theresa was an attractive older woman.

"Theresa?" Neily said quietly when she didn't show any notice that Neily had come into the room.

"Mikayla?" the older woman said when she did glance up.

"No, remember? It's Neily."

"Yes—Neily. I made that mistake again, didn't I?" the older woman said vaguely.

"Your grandson Wyatt is downstairs," Neily told her, watching closely for the woman's reaction.

It was another positive sign that Theresa brightened at that news—her eyes, her face, even her posture perked up.

"My Wyatt?" she repeated happily.

"And Mary Pat…"

"Mary Pat, too?" Theresa asked as if that were the frosting on the cake.

But then she sobered and became pensive again. "They haven't come to make me leave, have they? I can't go away from here. I won't. Not till I get what's mine!"

"I know. And, no, your grandson and Mary Pat aren't going to make you leave. They'll be staying here with you."

"They will?"

That sounded pleased and hopeful rather than fearful—something else Neily took note of.

"Will that be all right? For them to stay here in the house with you? Even if I leave?"

"Oh, yes. And they'll help me. I know they will. They'll help me get back what's mine. My Wyatt takes care of everything while Mary Pat takes care of me. They're very good to me, my little darlings."

"Would you like to come downstairs and say hello to them?"

"To Wyatt and Mary Pat and no one else?"

"Everyone else is gone. And the house looks so much better—you should see the good things that were done today while you were up here."

"I'd like to see Wyatt and Mary Pat."

"Let's go down then."

Theresa had no problem rising from the rocking chair or accompanying Neily down the steps. And the moment she caught sight of her grandson and caregiver, she passed Neily to hurry into the living room and hug them both like a child thrilled to see her loving parents after a separation. Clearly the older woman had no fear of either Wyatt Grayson or Mary Pat Gordman. It helped to confirm for Neily what the Missoula caseworker had said—that it was okay to turn Theresa's daily care over to them again while her situation, living conditions and ability to live at least somewhat independently were looked into.

"Oh, my dears, my dears! I'm so glad to see you!" Theresa was gushing. "But, Wyatt, where are Mikayla and the baby? Didn't you bring them? I still haven't seen that baby!"

Neily's interest got even stronger as she watched Wyatt Grayson's expression tense before he said, "Remember, Gram—Mikayla and the baby died."

Theresa pressed her fingertips to her cheeks on both sides of her face. "I'm sorry! I forgot again. I'm sorry, Wyatt, I'm sorry."

"Me, too. But it's all right. We're just glad we found you. You gave us all the scare of our lives."

"I had to get back here," Theresa confided as if she were telling a secret. "This is where I was born, you know," she added, motioning to their surroundings.

"We knew you were born in a small town near Billings," Wyatt said. "But that was all you ever told us. We didn't know the name of the town or that you still owned a house here."

"The lawyer pays the taxes. I think he pays to have someone look after it, too. Grampa had it arranged that way for me years and years ago and it's been happening automatically ever since. But I needed to come back now. I *needed* to, Wyatt!" Theresa said, suddenly sounding desperate and on the verge of getting upset.

"It's okay, Gram. We're just relieved that you're safe."

"Safe. I'm safe. I'm a bad person—you don't even know it—but I'm safe…"

Neily had seen this happen several times the last few days—Theresa drifting off while talking, things creeping into what she was saying that didn't make sense. In her brief experience Neily had already learned when that happened, talking to the older woman any further was futile. Pressing her only agitated her and nothing concrete or informative could be garnered from that point on.

Her grandson must have known that himself because he didn't push her.

Like a small child, Theresa moved to Mary Pat's side then, looping her arm through the nurse's. "I want to go to bed now. Will you read to me while I fall asleep, Mary Pat?"

The nurse patted Theresa's arm, tucked her in closer to her bulky side, and said, "I brought the book we started last week."

"I hope you didn't read any without me."

"Not a word," the nurse assured her.

Wyatt told Mary Pat that he would bring in her suitcase while she was getting his grandmother to bed, then he said to Theresa, "I'll come up and say good-night in a few minutes."

"Yes, in a few minutes," Theresa echoed before the nurse took her upstairs.

Neily and Wyatt Grayson watched Theresa and her nurse until they were out of sight.

"So," Theresa's grandson said then. "Are we all just going to be housemates?"

Neily turned to face him, recalling again how bad she looked and wishing even more, now that they were alone, that she'd somehow miraculously gotten cleaned up in the last few minutes.

"I won't be staying now that you're here. I'll be leaving Theresa to you and Mary Pat," she told him.

"We've at least passed muster that far?" he asked with a wry smile that—as difficult as it was for Neily to believe—made him even more drop-dead handsome.

Before she could answer, he said, "I know that once something like this has happened with a person who can't take care of themselves, and Human Services has been called in, the situation and the people involved are called into question. I'm not thrilled about it, but we don't have anything to hide and you're just doing what you have to. We all want the same thing—what's best for my grandmother."

That attitude made Neily's job much easier and she appreciated that.

"That *is* all we want," she confirmed.

"And for now you think it's best if we stay in Northbridge?"

"Theresa seems to have worked pretty hard to get here."

"I'll say. Ordinarily we have trouble convincing her to leave her house in Missoula. And she *never* leaves home alone. She hasn't in years. She also hasn't driven a car in years—I'm surprised she remembered how to do that. Of course, like I said, we still can't believe she did any of this."

"But now that she has, she feels strongly about staying here. I've conferred with the caseworker in Missoula and the Northbridge doctor who's examined your grandmother, and we all agree that for the time being it's probably better not to rock the boat."

"We don't have a problem with that. Whatever makes Gram happy, we'll accommodate."

"Good."

"But you won't be staying?"

"No, but I'll visit every day until we get this all sorted out."

"Fair enough. Anything you'd like to ask me now?"

Who Mikayla was and how she and a baby died...

But Neily wasn't sure if that really pertained to Theresa, so she refrained. "It's late. You probably want to settle in. And I'm wearing at least an inch of the dust and dirt we cleaned up around here today, so I think everything I need to discuss with you can wait."

"We," he repeated. "I saw that big group of people coming out as Mary Pat and I were coming in—were they part of that cleanup?"

"They're people who live around here. They all came in today to help out."

"Can I pay them?" Wyatt asked.

"That's not how things like this are done in Northbridge—when there's a need, people lend a hand to help out."

"That's really nice," he said with a surprised arch of those eyebrows again.

"It *is* nice," she agreed.

Then she caught herself staring too intently at him and decided it really was time to leave.

"I'll just get my overnight bag from the den," she said, clueless as to why her voice had suddenly gone quiet.

"I don't have any idea what the layout of this place is, but it looks pretty large from outside. Couldn't you have taken a bedroom upstairs?"

"There are five bedrooms upstairs, so, yes, I could have. But I couldn't take the chance that Theresa might slip out so I slept downstairs. With one eye open most of the time," she added with a weary laugh.

"I'm sorry," he apologized again. "I really would have gotten here before if I could have."

"It's all right. You're here now and after a shower, my own bed will feel that much better tonight."

And why did it seem so risqué to be talking about her bed to this man?

Once again, Neily had no answer for what was going on with her except maybe that she *was* really tired. Maybe that caused some kind of weird vulnerability to hunks from out of town.

She gave him her business card, and he gave her his cell-phone number. As they left the living room and crossed the entry to the den, she offered a brief summary of the layout of the house.

Then she grabbed her overnight bag from the den and took it with her to the front door.

"I would have been able to rest better tonight even here," she said, "because today I had our local contractor put keyed dead bolts on the front and back doors, and locks on the windows, too, to keep Theresa from slipping out—just in case." Neily handed over several keys. "As long as Theresa doesn't have access to these you shouldn't have to lose any sleep over that now."

"I at least want to pay for whatever materials were used," Wyatt said at her mention of the dead bolts.

"I'll let everyone know that."

"And please let them know how grateful I am—"

"That, too."

Neily opened the oversize front door to go out.

"I should get our suitcases and then lock us all in," Wyatt Grayson said, following her onto the porch.

But once they were in the cool late-evening air he

glanced around at the now quiet street and apparently realized that his SUV was the only vehicle in sight. "Where's your car?" he asked.

"I walked."

"Let me take you home, then," he said insistently and as if he should have somehow known that and offered earlier.

"Thanks, but it's a short walk and I'm sure you want to get back to your grandmother." And Neily was looking forward to a stroll through the cool spring air, hoping it would clear her head of the image of his eyes changing color almost like a hologram....

They both walked out into the yard. "I'll be back tomorrow," Neily said. "But if you need anything or have any questions before I get back, don't hesitate to call—middle of the night or not."

"Thanks."

Neily headed away from the house as Wyatt went to the SUV parked in the driveway. And while there was no call for it, she found herself glancing over her shoulder at him one last time.

He'd opened the rear of the vehicle and was hoisting luggage, his big, muscular body not straining in the slightest.

And at the sight of it, Neily's mouth went dry.

This is a first, she thought.

In her years as a social worker she'd felt compassion, pity, commiseration, sympathy, empathy, sadness, even grief and anger in conjunction with the people she'd dealt with.

But what had just happened with Wyatt Grayson had never happened to her before.

Never—ever—had she felt some kind of…

What?

Surely it couldn't be attraction.

And yet when he glanced over his shoulder at her as if he couldn't help himself either, something warm and bright flip-flopped in the pit of her stomach.

That couldn't go on! she told herself.

But still her hand rose in a wave that almost felt flirtatious.

A wave he returned.

The same way…

Chapter Two

Wyatt was sitting in bed early Monday morning when he flipped his cell phone closed to end the conference call he'd just had with his brother, Ry, and his sister, Marti. They were both in transit—Ry from Canada and Marti from Mexico—but they'd been eager to know that their grandmother was okay. They'd also wanted to touch base with Wyatt about where things stood in the investigation of the family by the Department of Public Health and Human Services now that Theresa had been formally tagged as a person unable to care for herself.

After filling them in and answering their questions in regards to the caseworker they'd be dealing with in Missoula and the one he would now be working with in Northbridge, he was having some trouble getting that Northbridge caseworker out of his head.

And not only because Neily Pratt would be taking her turn at scrutinizing him.

The fact that his grandmother had mistaken the social worker for his late wife, Mikayla, was not a coincidence. There was a resemblance. Not a strong one, but if Mikayla had had a cousin, Neily Pratt could have been it.

The hair color was the biggest similarity—thick, lustrous russet-brown hair so deep and rich a hue it demanded attention. And there was something about the nose—thin and pert. And cute. It was just a first-glance sort of resemblance, but it was still there.

But unlike Mikayla's sun-kissed skin, Neily Pratt was all peaches-and-cream. And she was shorter than Mikayla—even if Mikayla had ever worn the kind of tennis shoes the caseworker had had on.

Neily Pratt wasn't as voluptuous as Mikayla had been either, although she did have curves enough for him to take notice of. And there was a big difference in their eyes, too. Mikayla's had been hazel. Neily Pratt's were a deep metallic blue that glimmered so beautifully he'd had trouble not staring into them.

Which he didn't want to still be thinking about this morning.

Yet he couldn't help himself.

And that shook him up a little.

But then his entire encounter with the social worker had shaken him up a little. And not because he was alarmed to be under the investigation of Human Services—he knew there was no abuse or neglect of his grandmother to be found because there was no abuse or neglect. But something had stirred in him the night before in response to Neily Pratt. Something that had him looking forward to seeing her again, to seeing her all cleaned up, to talking to her.

And that did alarm him. Because those stirrings could be the beginning of things he didn't want to have anything to do with.

He shook his head and dropped it back to the headboard, disgusted with himself.

Why was this happening? He didn't even know this woman. And he sure as hell didn't *want* it to be happening. Not after what he'd gone through over Mikayla. Not after the last two years since her death.

Those two years had been beyond rough. They'd been so bad he'd worried that he wouldn't ever see emotional daylight again. So bad that he'd worried that he might end up in the grip of the kind of depression that had a hold of his grandmother.

But somehow—he wasn't sure exactly how or why—things had begun to smooth out. Slowly he'd realized that he *was* seeing emotional daylight. Only glimmers of it, yet even that had been such a relief, such a godsend, that he'd come to the conclusion that while life on his own might not be the way he'd thought things would be, the way he'd planned it, he didn't ever— *ever*—want to risk falling into that darkness again. The darkness that came with the loss of someone he was devoted to.

The surest way to avoid it, he'd decided, was to stay on his own. Not to let anyone else get so close that losing her—either in death or just through things not working out—could put him anywhere near that darkness again. He'd decided that for the sake of his own mental health, it was better to accept things as they were.

So that was what he'd done—he'd accepted it. Then he'd found some small pleasures, some enjoyment to go with it. Just not with another woman.

Which was his plan for the future. Stay solo—that was it in a nutshell. And he was committed to it. Because a little transient loneliness, having his sister and brother and grandmother be the only family he had, was still better than what he'd been through since Mikayla.

It was still better than taking any risk of ending up like his grandmother.

And staying solo had been working for him. No other woman had so much as caught his eye or his interest, let alone stirred anything in him.

Until last night.

So, yes, he would have preferred it if he *wasn't* looking forward to seeing the Northbridge social worker again.

Although he still didn't understand why he *was*.

Maybe it was the resemblance to Mikayla. Neily Pratt wasn't the spitting image of her but, still, maybe the resemblance was enough to trigger something in him.

But regardless of what was causing his eagerness to

see her again, he was damn well going to fight it with everything he had.

"So make it quick," he said aloud, as if he were giving the caseworker an order.

But he honestly hoped her work here would be done fast.

The faster the better.

And that then they wouldn't have to have anything to do with each other.

Because nothing was worth risking being on the edge of that dark pit again.

"She's having a sad day. Wyatt is sitting with her on the sunporch."

Thanks to a hectic schedule, Neily didn't get to the Hobbs house until late Monday afternoon. Mary Pat answered the door and let her in, informing her of Theresa's mood and whereabouts once they'd exchanged greetings.

"I'll go on back," Neily said. "I know the way."

The sunporch Mary Pat had referred to had probably been a greenhouse when the Hobbs place was built. It was a small space at the rear of the house, completely enclosed in glass—including overhead. Until the previous day's fix-up it had had more broken windows than not, but those had been replaced and it was once again sealed off from the elements. So even with only the not-too-intense April sunshine to warm it, it was still a comfortable spot from which to look down over a portion of town.

That was what Theresa and Wyatt seemed to be doing when Neily reached the doorway.

She refrained from announcing herself, wanting to observe any interactions between the two before either of them knew she was there.

They were sitting in old wicker chairs facing away from Neily but angled just enough toward each other that she had profile views of them both. Theresa's sadness was obvious—she sat with her head slumped, her expression gloomy, staring through the windows while Wyatt Grayson seemed to be trying to lift her spirits with a humorous story about a power-tool salesman.

There was nothing alarming in what Neily was seeing and yet she stayed quiet for a moment longer, her focus on Theresa's grandson.

She told herself that her interest was only professional, that it had nothing whatsoever to do with the fact that the guy was just too handsome to believe even dressed in a pair of plain tan twill slacks and a plaid shirt. It was his attitude toward his grandmother that she was observing, not the broad shoulders or the sun streaked through the dark-blond hair that gilded his starkly chiseled face.

But she couldn't fault his attitude any more than she could ignore his good looks, and after watching him actually win a small smile from Theresa, Neily could tell that there was no tension between the two.

"Knock-knock," she said from the doorway as if she'd just gotten there.

Wyatt Grayson immediately glanced in her direction,

his gray eyes bright and alert as his grandmother merely continued staring blankly out the windows in front of them.

"Look who's here, Gram—Neily," he said, getting to his feet.

Theresa didn't respond but still Neily went into the sunporch. "This is a nice place to be on a spring day," she said cheerily.

"It really is," Wyatt agreed the same way, as if it might inspire some enthusiasm from his grandmother. "It took some convincing but Mary Pat and I finally got Gram to come down and see for herself."

Still nothing from Theresa, as if she was too lost in her own thoughts to even hear what they were saying.

Wyatt Grayson stepped between the chairs and came toward Neily. "I don't suppose you're here to see me so I should probably give you some time alone with our girl. But could I have a minute when you're through?"

"Sure," Neily agreed, trying not to pay any attention to the little thrill of excitement she felt at the thought that he wanted a minute with her.

"Can I get you something in the meantime? Tea? Coffee?" he asked.

"No, thanks. Theresa is all I need," she answered.

"I'll get out of the way then," he said, reaching over the back of his grandmother's chair to squeeze her shoulder. "That's okay, isn't it, Gram? If I leave you with Neily?"

Theresa's only response was to pat his hand before her own fell limply back into her lap, all without glancing away from the windows.

Neily slipped between the wicker chairs and sat in the one he'd vacated. "We'll be fine."

He left then, but the heat of his big body lingered to warm the chair and Neily tried not to think about that— or like it—as she settled in.

"Hi, Theresa," she said. "How are you doing?"

Theresa shrugged but didn't answer, returning her gaze out the windows.

Neily checked the view, finding that the room looked down over an area of Northbridge that had been the first concentrated housing development in the late 1950s.

Finding nothing particularly noteworthy in that, she focused on Theresa instead.

"How do you like having your grandson and Mary Pat here?" Neily asked conversationally.

"They're good to me," Theresa answered without inflection.

"So you're glad that they're with you?"

"Yes."

"What does Mary Pat do for you?" Neily inquired, still making certain that her questions sounded like a friendly chat rather than a probe into Theresa's relationships.

The older woman shrugged. "Mary Pat does everything. She brings me my medicines when it's time to take them. Fixes my food. Tells me when it's cold and I should wear a sweater. Reminds me to brush my teeth or comb my hair when I forget. She's my mother hen." Theresa said all this in a flat tone of voice, never looking away from the windows.

"And yet you took her car keys and left her behind."

"I had to. I had to come here. Even without Mary Pat."

Neily heard Theresa's belligerence threatening and so veered away from the subject. "What about your grandson? What kind of things does he do for you?"

Another shrug. "Wyatt, Marti, Ry—I don't know what I'd do without them."

"Marti is Wyatt's sister?"

"Yes, and Ry is my other grandson, Wyatt's brother."

"They all visit you? Take care of you?"

"They worry about me. Fuss over me. Poor things—they could stay away but they don't. They treat me like a queen. And here I am, causing them more trouble."

"Have they said that? That you cause them trouble?"

"They never would. Whatever I want—that's what they always say. That's what they always do."

"But you didn't think they would this time? When you wanted to come to Northbridge?"

Theresa frowned. "I couldn't tell them what I did," she whispered.

Tears filled her eyes for a moment before she herself changed the subject this time, pointing in the direction of the houses that stretched out below them. "All of that belonged to my family, you know," she said.

"All of what, Theresa?"

"The land where those houses are now."

"No, I didn't know that," Neily said.

"Once upon a time, it was all Father's. Then it came to me…"

"Really?" Neily wondered if there was any truth to

this or if Theresa was drifting into one of her fantasies, the way she sometimes did. "I hadn't heard that but I imagine it would have been a long time ago that you…what? Sold the land?"

Theresa didn't answer; she merely went on staring down at the houses.

Neily tried again. "Is that what you want back— your land? Your father's land?"

If Theresa heard her, she didn't show it. Instead she said, "It was all ours. From here as far as you can see. Seems like so many things in life get lost."

"Did you *lose* the land somehow?"

Again there was no indication that Theresa had heard her.

Instead the older woman said, "Loss…so much loss. Wyatt knows what that's like. Marti, too."

Neily tried yet another tack. "I'm sorry for whatever losses you've suffered, Theresa. Do you want to talk about them?"

"I don't want to talk anymore," she said, pushing herself to her feet then. "I need to rest."

As if she were alone in the room, Theresa wandered out of it without another word.

Still, as far as Neily was concerned she'd accomplished her goal for today—to see if there had been any negatives to the arrival of Theresa's caregiver and her grandson. There hadn't been, so Neily followed the older woman out of the sunroom.

Mary Pat must have been watching for Theresa because the nurse joined her charge the minute Theresa reached the hall. Mary Pat tried to convince Theresa not to return to her bedroom, to go into the kitchen for tea instead. But Theresa insisted she needed to lie down, and the caregiver went along. Neily trailed them to the front of the house.

"That was quick."

Wyatt Grayson's voice came from the living room as Neily watched Theresa and Mary Pat climb the stairs. She turned to find him leaning negligently—and sexily—against the side of the archway, his hands slung in his pants pockets like a rodeo cowboy. It was slightly alarming that she could be struck all over again by the sight of him, but she was.

Still, she ignored the impact he kept having on her and said, "It *was* kind of quick, but I'll take what I can get."

"So maybe I can have *two* minutes instead of one?"

Surely he wasn't flirting with her. But if he wasn't, why was he smiling in such an enticing way?

Neily reminded herself that she was there on business, no matter *how* he smiled, and checked her watch. "I suppose I can spare *two* minutes before I'm due at my next home visit," she conceded. "But if you need more—"

"Two will do," he said. Then he got to the point— canceling the impression that he was flirting. "First I just wanted to say how much I appreciate everything that was done here—over breakfast this morning Gram was talking about broken glass and backed-up plumbing, about dust billowing out of the heating vents, about grime everywhere… Anyway, we got an even better idea of what kind of shape the place was in before yesterday and how much work had to have gone into getting it to this point, and I just had to say thanks again."

"You're welcome," Neily said simply.

"I was thinking that maybe we could have a thank-you dinner for everyone who pitched in, but I don't have any idea how to invite whoever that was."

"If you name a day and time I can take care of it," Neily offered. She didn't care about herself, but she was glad that he wanted to show his gratitude to the rest of the volunteers.

"You'll see to it that everyone involved gets invited?" Wyatt asked.

"I will."

"Mary Pat and I were thinking maybe Wednesday night? Seven o'clock?"

"Okay."

"Which brings me to my second question—I need to do some shopping for the dinner and to stock the house with more staples for us, too. Where do you do that around here? I didn't see any kind of supermarket or—"

"No, there isn't any kind of supermarket but we have the Groceries and Sundries—it's reasonably well stocked. Plus there's a butcher shop, a bakery—specialty stores…" Then, from out of nowhere her mouth ran away with her and she heard herself say, "If you'd like I could show you where everything is tonight and you could do some shopping—"

"That would be great," he said before she could finish. Then, as if he, too, had spoken before thinking, he added, "If you're sure. If your time is already stretched too thin or you had other plans —"

"I just have one more home visit and then I'm free," she said, all the while telling herself to use one of the excuses he was giving her and not go through with something that *wasn't* part of her job.

But did she backpedal and get herself out of what she knew she shouldn't do?

No, she didn't. Instead she got in deeper. "Most things are open until about eight. I could run home after this next appointment, grab a quick bite to eat, and be back at six-thirty or so…"

"Terrific—a tour by a native. That should give me the ins and outs."

"Maybe you could persuade Theresa to go with us," Neily said then, thinking that getting the older woman to leave the house *would* put this back in the realm of work.

"I'll ask," Wyatt said. "But no one will be more surprised than me if she goes."

"Maybe if Mary Pat comes along, too?" Neily suggested.

Apparently that had been transparent because Wyatt's smile turned quizzical. "Are you afraid to be alone with me? Because I'm harmless…"

Harmless maybe, but definitely not charmless.

"No, I'm not afraid to be alone with you." She was afraid of these strange things that came to life in her when she was. "I just thought it would be good for all of you to see Northbridge and learn your way around."

"I'll do what I can to persuade Gram but I wouldn't count on it. And if Gram stays, Mary Pat stays."

Neily nodded. "Well, six-thirty one way or another then?"

"I'll be ready. Unless you tell me how to get to your place and let me pick you up…"

"It's just easier if I come get you." Because then she could have the control and it could seem more like work than a…

A *date?*

No, this definitely was not—in any way—a date!

Then why was she so nervous?

To cover that up, she looked at her watch again and said, "I really should get going. I can guarantee that my next stop won't be quick."

Wyatt nodded, pushed away from the wall and went to the front door to open it for her, smiling still as if she'd thoroughly entertained him.

"I'll see you tonight," he said, his gray eyes never wavering from her.

"Tonight," Neily confirmed. But for no reason she understood, she ducked her head bashfully as she passed in front of him to go.

And as she got into her car, she discovered that there was a small part of her that hoped that Theresa and Mary Pat *would* stay home tonight.

Chapter Three

Neily was well aware that when she'd met Wyatt Grayson Sunday night she'd been a mess, and that when she'd seen him earlier Monday afternoon she'd had a full day's wear and tear on her clothes, hair and makeup. She wanted to improve on those two impressions the third time he saw her, so she skipped dinner Monday evening in order to devote every minute to her appearance before picking him up.

But it was only for her own sake, she told herself. For her own sense of self-esteem. Something about the man unnerved her in a way no one had ever unnerved her in the past. She had five brothers, for crying out loud—she hadn't even been that awkward around boys when she'd been a girl. Yet there she'd been this afternoon, sounding like a shy kid.

And that just wouldn't do. Especially not when she was in the position of judging Wyatt Grayson's stability, his character, his demeanor. She needed some stability of her own, some sense of decorum and authority. None of that was conveyed by presenting herself looking like a chimney sweep or in her geeky teenager imitation today.

So tonight she was going to make sure she looked…good. But not to wow Wyatt Grayson. She was just trying to amend the two previous messages she may have sent.

There clearly wasn't any reason to try to wow Wyatt Grayson anyway, she told herself as she changed into a fitted cashmere turtleneck sweater and the leg-lengthening, hip-slimming pinstriped slacks that she usually referred to as her first-date pants. There was no reason at all to try to wow him. He was an integral part of a case she was handling and that made any personal involvement a conflict of interest.

Yes, he was great-looking and charming, but there were a lot of great-looking, charming guys in Northbridge who didn't do anything for her.

Even so, there was no denying that something about being around Theresa's grandson had turned her into an airhead this afternoon and no matter what that something was, she had to get a grip on it and stop it.

"Stop it in its tracks!" she said to herself as she powdered her nose and applied some blush and mascara. Then she took her hair down from the clip that held it and brushed it before using a very large curling iron to smooth it and curve the ends under her chin.

But getting a grip on herself and on the weird effects caused by Wyatt Grayson didn't worry her. Now that she knew that a simple touch of his hand or a little conversation or just being around him could knock her for a loop, she knew to go in steeled against it. And once she was steeled and ready for anything, there was no getting to her—that was something that being tormented by five brothers had prepared her for.

"So you're nothing but another case to me, Grayson," she said out loud as she finished with the curling iron and combed her hair to fall silkily around her face.

Besides, tonight she would have the advantage of being in her car, of walking around her town. And while they were in *her* car and walking around *her* town, her only goal was to do *her* job. To subtly get to know the man solely in his role as Theresa's grandson in order to determine if he was a fit caretaker and guardian for the older woman.

Which meant that this was absolutely *not* a date.

Even if she *did* have first-date-like butterflies in her stomach to go with her first-date pants.

"You must think I'm an idiot," Wyatt said later that evening as he and Neily sat at one of the bistro tables in the new coffee emporium that had just opened in Northbridge.

Neily took a sip of the hot chocolate they'd just been

served. "Why?" she asked, having no clue what he was talking about.

"I drove up this street when I came in last night. I didn't know it was all there was of Northbridge or that I hardly needed a tour guide to navigate it."

Neily gave him a mock frown. "Are you calling us a one-horse town? Because we're so much more than that. We're a one-*T* town—there's Main Street that runs north and south to South Street, which goes east to west to make the *T*. Turn left on South Street at the town square and you get to the college and the houses and farms and ranches in that direction. Or turn right on South Street to go to your place and the outlying houses, farms and ranches in that direction—"

"And don't forget those four cross streets along Main—they're teeming with at least six or eight stores and businesses," he added, playing along.

"Plus we have a stoplight and now even this coffee shop," she reminded.

"Just one coffee shop and just one stoplight, but who's counting? You're practically a metropolis."

Again she pretended affront. "Didn't you get everything you needed tonight?"

"I did," he conceded over his own cup. "Although I noticed that there's a lumberyard but not much in the way of a hardware store."

"Did you want something more than the nuts and bolts they sell at the Groceries and Sundries?"

"No, it was purely a professional observation."

"You're the hardware police?" she asked, joking still.

"No, not the hardware police, but you do know we're Home-Max, don't you?"

He didn't seem to be kidding anymore so Neily said, "Really? Home-Max?"

"Really—Home-Max. I take it you've heard of us?"

Home-Max was the chain of large warehouselike stores that sold all manner of building materials, lumber, home-improvement and remodeling supplies, large and small appliances, everything pertaining to lighting, lamps and wiring, as well as garden, patio, barbecue and landscaping equipment and machinery. The company had been in the news lately for sweeping the Western states with openings of new stores and doing newsworthy damage to their competitors.

"Of course I've heard of Home-Max, but, no, I didn't know *you*—personally—*are* Home-Max."

"Well, my family is," he clarified. "My sister, Marti, my brother, Ry, Gram and I own them all."

"Theresa didn't tell me that," Neily said as the information sank in.

"It isn't as if she's involved, and half the time she forgets that it *is* Home-Max now. She knew it as G and H Hardware—that was how it started, with my grandfather's one-corner hardware store."

"Your grandfather—Theresa's husband," Neily said to clarify.

"Right. He had the hardware store when they met. Just a small place he ran by himself. Gram had a little money and after they were married she put it into the store to expand it—that's when it became G and H: *G* for Grayson, *H* for Hobbs, Gram's maiden name, since Hobbs money provided for the expansion. When my grandfather died, the store went to my father—their only child. Things boomed with him in charge, and over the years Dad opened six other G and H Hardwares. We all worked them as soon as we were old enough. But when our mom and dad were killed in a car accident eight years ago, Marti and Ry and I were left in the hot seat."

"How so?"

"The builder's-warehouse type of stores had begun to hurt us. Business was dwindling, and we had a fair offer to buy us out."

"Why didn't you sell?"

"Mainly because of Gram. She hasn't always been as bad as she is but her problems weren't too much better eight years ago than they are now—she needed live-in care, and that's expensive. The offer to buy us out wouldn't have left her with enough to provide for that indefinitely, and if Marti and Ry and I went our separate ways, working for other people, we couldn't be sure we'd be able to afford to make up the difference over time. And the thought of having to institutionalize Gram... Well, we didn't want that. So we decided to gamble. To play *with* the big boys rather than sell out to them. We closed all but one of our stores, and turned the only remaining G and H Hardware into the first Home-Max. Then we went from there. And it just worked out."

Neily was sure he was making it sound less complicated and stressful than it had been.

"You must have always been close to Theresa to risk everything for her sake."

He shrugged. "Pretty close, yeah. And we just wanted what was best for her. Plus it seemed only fair that—since her money had helped begin things—we do whatever we could to keep them going. But it wasn't for her sake alone. Marti, Ry and I wanted to go on working together, so it was for our sakes, too. We were all just lucky that we made it."

Still Neily thought it was admirable that Theresa's family had considered her contribution and made her welfare a priority. Neily was also impressed that rather than taking the easy way out of caring for a grandmother with special needs, Wyatt and his siblings hadn't cut and run when the opportunity to do that had presented itself.

The more she learned about Wyatt, the more she leaned away from any thoughts of neglect.

And toward liking him.

They both had another drink of their hot chocolates before Neily decided to use his mention of Theresa as her opening to talk about the older woman. And keep herself from thinking things about Wyatt Grayson that she didn't want to be thinking.

"So even eight years ago Theresa was basically in the shape she's in now?"

He nodded, a sad, sober expression on his handsome face. "Gram has had mental-health issues as long as I can remember. She gets into severe depressions. She has times when she's out of touch with reality, delusional—that's happening more often as she ages. She was always fearful, and that developed into full-blown phobias—those are what started her being housebound and needing round-the-clock care, and why none of us can understand her doing what she did to get here."

"And the memory issues?"

"Those are getting worse, especially her short-term memory. Sometimes she thinks that things that happened decades ago were just yesterday, and she forgets what *did* happen yesterday. She's really a tortured soul."

"Does she have a specific diagnosis?"

"A laundry list of them. And she's on medications to treat them all, which helps to some extent. She's also had therapy, but nothing has made a huge improvement."

"I'm assuming the possibility of early abuse has been looked into?" Neily said.

"She's denied that there was any of that. She makes her childhood sound perfect. Happy. She frequently says that she was the apple of her parents' eyes, how much she loved them, how devastated she was when they died. I know that losing my grandfather caused more deterioration, and then losing my father brought on more still, so maybe there's something to that."

"And even when she talked about her perfect childhood she didn't tell you anything about Northbridge or that she still had the house here?" Neily asked, finding it curious that Theresa had been so secretive about that.

Wyatt shook his head. "Like I said before, the only mention of *where* she grew up was a generality."

"So she didn't tell you that her family—her father—had owned land here?"

That seemed to surprise him. "No. You mean her father owned more than the house?"

"She told me today that he—and then she—owned the section of land you can see from the sunporch, where there are houses now."

"Do you think it's true?"

Neily shrugged. "I've never heard that, but it isn't as if I would have heard about who owned land twenty years before I was born. I was just wondering if maybe that should be looked into. If it's true, maybe that's what she thinks she can reclaim."

"Maybe that's what was taken from her, you mean? Do you think someone stole it from her or swindled her?"

Neily shrugged again. "I don't know. I suppose old land records could be checked into."

Wyatt's expression had gone from sad to intrigued. "Want to play detective with me?"

Neily laughed. "I don't think that's in my job description."

"Might be fun, though," he said with an alluring wiggle of his eyebrows.

Too alluring.

Neily reminded herself that she was supposed to be steeled against his charm. But apparently even early practice steeling herself against whatever her brothers threw her way was not enough when it came to resisting Wyatt Grayson.

Both of their cups were empty by then and noticing

that seemed like an aid to her cause. Rather than respond to Wyatt's it-might-be-fun-to-play-detective-with-him, she said, "We should probably go."

Wyatt didn't immediately agree. He went on looking at her, smiling as if he was enjoying the view. But he didn't push the suggestion that she help investigate old land records and after a moment he stood and held her chair while she stood, too.

He'd already paid for their hot chocolates, and now he tossed a tip onto the table before he followed Neily out of the shop.

Don't let him get to you, she told herself on the way to her car, which was parked at the curb a few doors down.

She slid in behind the wheel and started the engine as Wyatt slipped into the passenger seat. It didn't help that when he did, he angled toward her and stretched his arm across the back of her seat. It also didn't help that he was a big man and that he seemed to fill the interior of the car with hundred-proof testosterone.

"So what do you say?" he asked as she headed for South Street. "Will you help me out? I know North-bridge is small and you can probably just point out where I'd find land records, but you also probably know the city clerk—or whoever handles that kind of thing—and could make it easier for me to get access to whatever I need."

That was all true.

"You could think of it as helping Gram—that *is* in your job description, right?" he added.

"Right…"

Saying that made it sound as if she were wavering.

She *did* want to know all she could about Theresa and what was behind the older woman's flight to North-bridge. A complete picture *could* be helpful.

But it would mean spending more time alone with Theresa's grandson. And while they *had* talked about Theresa, and while talking to Wyatt *had* given Neily more insight into him and his relationship with his grand-mother—all of which qualified as information she needed to be gathering—she couldn't deny that tonight had seemed less like work and more like an evening with a handsome, easy-to-talk-to, amusing and entertaining man.

It had seemed more like the date she'd been insist-ing to herself it wasn't.

"Come on," he cajoled as she pulled into the drive-way of the Hobbs house. "Help me out. For Gram's sake. And for the sake of your whole one-*T* town."

Neily put the car into Park but left the engine running and glanced over at Wyatt. "For the sake of my whole one-*T* town?"

"What if some horrible, dastardly deed was done to Gram to wrench her land from her, and right in your midst is the rat who did it? Wouldn't you want to know? What if the rat is your mayor or someone in some position of power, doing more dastardly deeds behind the scenes without anyone knowing? He or she could be embezzling funds or pilfering retirement accounts or selling bogus city bonds—"

"Those would be dastardly deeds," Neily agreed with a laugh at his melodramatics.

"You are in charge of making sure any wrongs done against Gram are righted," he pointed out.

The kind of wrong he was talking about was out of her province, but still, Neily was curious about whether Theresa actually *had* been a victim of some kind of wrongdoing, or if her mental state was further deteriorating.

Which gave her a reason to grant Wyatt's request without admitting to herself that she kind of wanted to spend more time with him.

"All right," she said as if he'd worn her down. "I'll help you. But only to get a more complete picture of Theresa."

Wyatt smiled slowly, as if he was pleased regardless of what was behind her decision. "Tomorrow?"

"Theresa is on my calendar for every day. But I have a full schedule and you're last on it, so we'll barely make it to the courthouse before it closes. That won't leave us much time to look through land records."

"Later in the day is actually better for me. I have to make some business calls and I'd rather get them in before we go."

Neily nodded, knowing even as she did that the fact that she was already looking forward to the next day was a bad sign.

But she didn't back out.

"Thanks for showing us around tonight," he said then.

"Thanks for the hot chocolate," she countered.

Wyatt leaned forward and although there was absolutely no reason to believe it was even likely, Neily thought he was going to kiss her good-night.

Shocked, she bolted up straighter and veered away from him just as he pulled his bags of groceries from behind her seat, obviously having been intent on only that from the beginning.

Of course he hadn't been going to *kiss* her! Why would she ever have even thought that?

Wyatt settled his sacks on his lap and looked at her again, showing no sign that he'd noticed her overreaction.

"I'll see you tomorrow then?"

"You're my four-thirty."

Something about that garnered her a sweet, sexy smile.

"Shall I meet you somewhere?"

Maybe it *would* be better not to be in a car with him again.

"Records are all kept at the courthouse," she said, explaining to him where that was.

"I'll be there at four-thirty," he assured her when she was finished.

"I'll see you then."

Wyatt nodded and she expected him to get out. But instead he sat there a moment longer, looking at her, studying her.

Then he smiled again, a mystery-man smile if ever Neily had seen one, muttered "Good night" and finally slid from her passenger seat, closing the door after himself.

She should have immediately put the car into gear and backed out of the drive. But she didn't. She was too intent on watching the tall, well-built man carry his packages to the front door.

And despite the fact that she continued to remind

herself that this had not been a date, and to chastise herself for even fleetingly thinking he might have kissed her, she couldn't help fantasizing—just a little—about what it might have been like if it hadn't been grocery sacks he'd reached for.

If it had been her instead.

Chapter Four

After two taps on the front door of a farmhouse outside of Northbridge early Tuesday evening, Neily opened the door and stepped inside.

"Miss Sela, are you here? It's Neily."

"I can see that. It's you and some man," came a wheezy voice from a chair in a corner of the living room to the left.

"Yes, me and some man," Neily confirmed. "I just got an emergency call that you ran away from the hospital and no one knew where you were."

"I'm where I told them I wanted to be. You knew where to find me. Couldn't have been too hard for those numbskulls to figure out."

Neily closed the door behind herself and Wyatt, and then led the way into the musty-smelling living room.

Sitting up very straight in the wing chair was a tiny woman dressed in the clothes she'd been wearing when Neily had taken her to the hospital that morning—complete with the coat Neily had helped her into. Miss Sela's snow-white hair was neatly pulled into a ponytail, and from amidst her wan, wrinkled face pale-blue eyes were alert as she watched Neily and Wyatt join her.

"Miss Sela, this is Wyatt Grayson," Neily said courteously. "Wyatt, this is Miss Sela Knotts. Miss Sela, you might know Wyatt's grandmother—Theresa Hobbs—"

"Hobbs? 'Course I knew the Hobbses. I had my Thomas the same week Lurene had her daughter. Theresa—that'd be her, all right, but did you say she's this man's *grandmother?* Sheesh, I'm gettin' old."

"Miss Sela is ninety-six," Neily informed Wyatt.

"I guess if my Thomas had lived he could have been a grandfather to a grown man now," Miss Sela said, apparently having done the math. "I just always picture him the way he was when he died—lookin' like the two of you, too young to be a grandfather."

Neily and Wyatt had just arrived at the courthouse when she had received the panicked call about Miss Sela. Neily had needed to respond to the situation immediately, and he'd insisted on lending a hand finding her. So he had come along. Somewhat to Neily's dismay, because she'd found herself again in an enclosed car with him, his clean, woodsy-scented cologne going right to her head.

She sat on the edge of the sofa close to the elderly woman, while Wyatt remained standing at the opposite end of the couch.

"So what's going on, Miss Sela?" Neily asked.

"I wanted to be in my own house, sleep in my own bed. I told them that. They treated me like I was a two-year-old, talked to me as if I was stupid or deaf or both, and so I left."

"You have pneumonia, Miss Sela."

"I know that. But I can take the pills myself and I'll get better rest here than in that hospital. But would they listen? They wouldn't and I walked out. Hitched a ride home with Stan Lowell. Told him my car was in the shop. Nobody can keep me if I don't want to be kept," she concluded decisively.

Then, as if that closed the subject, the old woman looked at Wyatt and said, "Theresa Hobbs… Terrible, what happened to that family! Poor Theresa was just a girl when she lost her mama and her papa. They were comin' in from Billings—that was before anything could get done here, when a person had to go to the city to see a doctor or a dentist. Toothache, I think is what sent them to Billings that day. Got stuck in a blizzard halfway home. Found 'em frozen to death when the storm cleared."

"You're exactly right," Wyatt confirmed. "Some of that I just learned myself today, reading old newspapers at the library."

He sounded impressed with the woman's memory. Neily knew Sela Knotts's mind was still sharp, so it didn't surprise her. In fact, now that the old woman had brought up the subject of Theresa's family, Neily wondered what else Miss Sela remembered and said,

"We were at the courthouse to look up land records when the hospital called me. You wouldn't happen to know if Theresa's father owned some land...?"

"As a matter of fact, he did. A lot of it. Prime property that Theresa sold for a song to Hector Tyson. That miserable coot bragged about it after Theresa left town—went around with his chest out like the cock of the walk, saying what a good deal he'd gotten for himself. Then he turned around and made his millions selling off the lots and supplying all the materials to put up the houses there now. It's a shame—all that could have been that girl's. But Lurene and Herb doted on her and there she was—young and alone—I suppose she just wanted to sell and put this place behind her." Miss Sela shrugged. "Or maybe not, since she never did sell their house. And now what's this I've heard about her havin' to sneak into the place like a thief in the night?"

"It's true, she's come back," Neily said. "But not everyone is as rough and tumble as you are. Theresa has some problems and we're trying to figure out if there might be something we can do to help her with them."

"Well, don't send her to the damn hospital," Miss Sela said. "You let them get their hooks in you in those places and you're done for."

"But you need the treatments they can give you there to clear your lungs," Neily pointed out, picking up where they'd left off in regards to the elderly woman's health.

"Pish! I'm breathin', aren't I? I couldn't be talkin' to you if I wasn't."

"You're not breathing as well as you should be—I

can hear the tightness in your chest with every word. That's why I took you into the emergency room when I heard it this morning."

Miss Sela glared at her.

"What if I give you my absolute promise that if you let me take you back to the hospital it won't be for more than a few days? I know you ordinarily do just fine out here on your own, but for now that just isn't a good idea," Neily said. "You don't even *have* the pills you need to take—you left without them."

Miss Sela waved away that criticism. "I would have called to have 'em sent out to me. I know I need 'em."

"You also need a couple days of lying in a bed and being waited on, of being served meals that you haven't had to fix yourself."

"Doesn't take much to heat a can of soup," the old woman insisted.

"You'll get better and stronger faster, though, if you're eating more than that and not wearing yourself out moving around here," Neily said.

She could see that the elderly woman's adventure had taken its toll and Miss Sela was wilting in spite of herself. After a moment of scowling at her, Miss Sela said, "After a few days you'll pick me up yourself and bring me back here?"

"I promise. You know that I know that you do all right on your own, and there's no reason for that to change. But if *I* had pneumonia, chances are I'd have to be in the hospital myself. We do what we have to."

Miss Sela sighed, making a rattling sound in the

process, but Neily took that as concession and stood. "Come on before you make yourself sicker," she urged, moving to help the elderly woman up.

"I'll do it!" Miss Sela snapped at her. "'Bout the time you think I can't you'll be comin' at me with canes and walkers and wheelchairs and whatnot!"

But it was obvious she was too weak to get out of her chair.

That was when Wyatt stepped up. "It's been a while since I had a beautiful woman take my arm. Maybe you'd do me the honor?" he suggested, holding out an elbow to her.

Miss Sela accepted it, managing to rise from her chair that way.

"Not a lot of handsome young bucks get their arms around me these days," she said with an ornery chuckle as Wyatt helped her. Then, glancing at Neily, she added, "Don't get your feathers too ruffled, Neily, I'll return 'im when I'm finished with 'im."

Wyatt smiled and winked over the cottony head of hair and Neily couldn't help laughing at the two of them. And liking Wyatt just a tiny bit more.

The past weekend had marked the grand opening of the addition of a dine-in area to the local pizza parlor. There were signs for it all over town, and after readmitting Miss Sela to the hospital Wyatt persuaded Neily to share one of the new tables and a pizza with him.

It was a public place, after all, she reasoned. Maybe just being in the vicinity of other people would make her less aware of everything about the guy that seemed to draw her in. She *did* want to discuss what they'd just learned about Theresa's land, and at least she wouldn't be alone with Wyatt to do that.

So she left her car parked next to Wyatt's at the courthouse and they walked into the pizza parlor.

Unfortunately the only free table was in a quiet corner and the seating put them so close together that their knees kept bumping. And the knee bumping sent tingling sensations radiating up Neily's thighs every time.

But she tried to ignore it by focusing on the sole purpose for being with him in the first place—land records and solving the puzzle of Theresa.

"I guess Miss Sela saved us hours in the courthouse basement," Neily said after they'd ordered their pizza and been served iced tea. "Theresa's father—and then Theresa—*did* own the land."

Wyatt shrugged. "You just never know if what Gram says is going to prove true or not."

"But if that's what she considers *taken* from her, she can't get it back," Neily pointed out.

"*If* that's what she's talking about. Did it seem to you that it was?"

Neily sweetened her tea and took a sip, shrugging herself this time. "I don't know. She just sort of said it matter-of-factly. And she didn't say specifically that that was what she wanted back, no. But—"

"Who can tell," Wyatt finished for her. "It does seem likely that the money she made selling the land was what she invested in the hardware store."

"It would make sense since she didn't sell the house. Unless she inherited money or something else from her parents."

"She's never said anything that would lead us to think she inherited anything. I guess we never thought about where the money she invested in the business came from."

"Do you know what your great-grandfather did for a living?"

"He was a simple carpenter—that's the way Gram puts it. Since he *did* own the land he must have saved up to buy it or maybe bought it a plot at a time or hit on a particularly good deal or something, because I never had the impression that he was excessively well off. Even the house is more grand than I would have thought Gram grew up in, but when I asked her about that today she said her father had built the place himself, from the ground up."

"I can't imagine property was expensive that long ago in Northbridge—that probably helped him afford the land," Neily contributed.

After drinking some of his tea, Wyatt switched gears. "So who is this Hector Tyson? The way Miss Sela talked about him I figured you knew him and that he might even still be around."

"Yes, he's still around and I do know him. Everyone does. He's Northbridge's rich curmudgeon. Although it's interesting to find out that he *got* rich from what he did with your grandmother's land. I didn't know that before today."

"Where did you think he made his money?"

"He owns that lumberyard you thought was woefully inadequate in comparison to your Home-Max stores. Except for the few little things that the Groceries and Sundries carries, the lumberyard has always been the only local option for hardware or building supplies. Hector's prices are high but everyone pays them because—"

"It's the only game in town. Which makes it more convenient than traveling to Billings or having things sent from there," Wyatt guessed.

"Right. I just thought the price gouging was how he got rich."

"He's been around a long time, I take it?"

"Not as long as Miss Sela—he's eighty-four."

"So, about nine years older than Gram," Wyatt said. "Do you think he could have done something illegal to get the land away from her?"

Neily shrugged again. "The sale itself must have been legal for him to turn around and sell it himself. His ownership had to be recorded, the sale of each lot had to be registered, titles had to be awarded—it isn't as if he could have just taken it from Theresa and accomplished all that. Northbridge is a small town but everything is still done by the book."

Wyatt's eyebrows arched. "How about something legal but underhanded? Maybe he did something along those lines—I know that when I talked to Gram yesterday about why she came back here she made reference to a *he* but she wouldn't tell me who *he* was. She said *he* told her it would be all right, that she'd get over something."

"But if she was talking about Hector, what could he have done that was legal but underhanded?" Neily asked.

"Not being underhanded myself, I don't have any idea. I also can't say that this Hector guy is the man Gram was talking about—it could be someone else for all I know. Maybe we can get her to tell us more."

There was that *we* again, Neily noted.

Their salads arrived and she decided to use the interruption to branch off. "What was that you told Miss Sela about reading old newspapers at the library today?"

"I decided to see if anything had been written about Gram or her parents," he said after tasting his salad. "Selling the land must not have been newsworthy because there wasn't anything about that. Or about this Hector Tyson in conjunction with Gram. About all I found was her birth announcement and the story on the death of my great-grandparents."

"And you said Miss Sela was right about the trip to the dentist in Billings and freezing to death halfway home?"

"According to the paper," Wyatt said. "Gram was sixteen."

"Was that when she left Northbridge?" Neily asked.

"No, now that you mention it. That's always how I've heard it—she tells the story this way. Her parents died and she went to live with an aunt in Missoula. On the bus trip she met my grandfather, they hit it off, and she married him three months later on her eighteenth birthday. Until now, that's all any of us have ever known."

"But apparently there was a time lapse between when her parents died and when she left Northbridge? A year or so when she was here, on her own, at a young age?" Neily said, piecing it together.

"It looks like it," Wyatt confirmed, obviously as curious about that fact as it made Neily. "Gram never said that but that's how the time line works out—her parents died in mid-December, her birthday is in February, so she must have turned seventeen the February after their deaths. But she didn't leave for Missoula until three months before she turned eighteen."

"And you don't have any idea what—if anything—went on during that year or so—"

"Looks like it was about eleven months."

"During that eleven months when she was here on her own?" Neily asked.

"No idea at all. But it makes you wonder, doesn't it? Especially since during that time she sold this Hector Tyson prime property for a song—to quote Miss Sela," Wyatt said, sounding suspicious.

Their pizza arrived then, and as their waitress served the first slices Wyatt said, "I guess I have some digging to do."

Neily didn't know why but the *I* rather than the *we* in that this time disappointed her.

Wyatt finished chewing a bite of his own, then said, "So how did your life's work become little old ladies?"

Neily smiled at that. "It isn't as if they're my specialty. Geriatric case management is just part of the job.

A pretty small part, contrary to what it might seem. You just haven't seen me in action with anything else."

That had sounded flirty and she hadn't meant for it to. Even if she *had* been thinking about the fact that his eyes were picking up a bluish cast in the light of the restaurant…

He apparently hadn't missed her flirtatiousness because he gave her a delighted smile and said, "What other kind of action are you into?"

No, don't flirt back. I'll be sunk, she thought.

In a more appropriate tone, she said, "I cover all the bases for social work and counseling in Northbridge— being the only licensed social worker here."

"What does that involve?" he asked, his attention, his interest, completely on her. Which was particularly nice for Neily, who spent so much of her time listening to other people.

"I get called if there are reports of neglect or abuse of anyone. I make sure services—like home health care or food stamps or whatever—are available to people who need them. I've worked with families who've had their farms foreclosed on or need help because their homes were destroyed by fire. I do some private counseling—group, individual, marriage and family. I also provide services for the school—I assess learning and social-emotional disabilities, I run socialization skills groups for kindergartners—"

"Socialization skills for kindergartners? What do you need to do with that? Kids are kids. They play on the playground, they color, they—"

"They have issues like everyone," Neily said protectively, but not without a smile. "We talk about sharing and compromising and being empathetic. And we play games like Food-Not-Food—"

"Food-Not-Food?"

"I say, 'Pizza—food? Not food?' And if you're a kindergartner, you say…"

"'Pizza is food?'"

"Good," Neily praised with the same enthusiasm she used for her groups. "Then I say, 'Pencil erasers—food? Not food?'"

Wyatt laughed. "Not food," he said as if he was only admitting it reluctantly.

"So if you're five you have now learned not to eat your pencil eraser. Or other things I have to include that you don't even want to know about."

"Probably not," he said with another laugh that somehow made Neily realize in that moment how much she was enjoying herself. And being with him.

"So it definitely isn't just working with little old ladies," he conceded then. "But you do seem to have just the right touch with them, from what I've seen."

Neily didn't know why, but she couldn't help basking in his praise—something else she knew she shouldn't be doing, any more than she should be enjoying his company or having fun with him.

Luckily they'd finished their meal by then, and that gave her an out.

"I should get home. I haven't been there since before dawn this morning," she said suddenly.

"That *is* too long a workday," he agreed. "This has been nice for me, though. I hope it hasn't been too much like work for you."

It hadn't been anything like work—that was the problem...

"I think I've been off the clock for a while, but I should still get home," she said.

He paid the bill despite Neily's attempt to split it with him, and they retraced their steps to the courthouse parking lot.

"You said that you contacted everyone who worked on the house Sunday about the dinner tomorrow night, right?" Wyatt asked as they reached their cars.

"For the most part. But don't worry, I'm sure everyone I asked to tell someone else will have. You'll have a houseful," she assured him. She opened her door and stood in its lee, looking at him.

The parking lot was well lit, so she could see his face clearly. As she gazed up into it she was struck all over again by how gorgeous he was, by the fact that the more time she spent with him, enjoying his company, the more attractive she found him.

"Can I ask a favor?" Wyatt said into Neily's secret attempt not to be so bowled over by him.

"You can ask," she said. "But that doesn't mean I'll say yes."

Okay, flirty again. *Stop that!*

"Would you mind coming a little earlier than everyone else?"

So they could have a few minutes alone?

That was what flashed through her mind. What some part of her actually hoped he meant— —much as she knew it was out of line and unprofessional and totally unwise.

Then Wyatt qualified his request. "I don't know anyone who's coming and it would help if you were there to fill me in."

Which was, of course, all there was to it. All there should have been to it.

"Sure. No problem," Neily agreed airily, as if she wasn't warring with herself over thoughts and tiny budding feelings that she not only knew she shouldn't be having but didn't want to have.

Then, to remind herself that she had no business entering the realm of anything personal with this man, she said, "Do you think your grandmother will come out of the bedroom to see everyone? Because she wouldn't on Sunday."

Wyatt shook his handsome head. "I talked to her about it today but I'd say it's unlikely. The most I could get her to agree to is to think about it, but I wouldn't bet on her joining us. Even if we were at home and people she knew were coming to dinner there wouldn't be much of a chance that she'd leave her room."

"I'll want to visit with her even if she doesn't, since I missed today."

"She'll be glad to see you. Like I said before, she likes you. She talks about you and seems eager to see you again. She's just never good about socializing— maybe you could do socialization skills group with her."

He was teasing her and Neily couldn't help smiling up at him. "Food-Not-Food?"

"I think she has that down," he said with an answering smile that put creases at the corners of his eyes and in the centers of both cheeks.

And that was when their gazes seemed to lock and hold.

Then her view took in his mouth and it was kissing that was on her mind.

But not in any sort of shocked, panicked way, like the previous night when she'd mistaken his reaching for his grocery bags for a move to kiss her.

Tonight was different. Kissing was on his mind, too—she knew it as surely as if she were reading words on a page.

This might not have qualified as a date any more than the time they'd spent together the previous night had, but it still *felt* like one. Like a really great date, the kind where two people hit it off.

And *had* this been a really great second date, a goodnight kiss would have been the natural course of events.

Which might have been why she discovered herself leaning ever so slightly forward, her chin tipped ever so slightly upward.

Which might also have been why Wyatt seemed to be inching ever so slightly toward her…

Before he stopped.

He straightened up. He cocked his head in a way that indicated he was asking himself what he was doing, and no kiss was forthcoming.

To Neily's relief.

And dismay.

"I'll let you get home," Wyatt said, his voice more quiet than it had been.

"Yeah. You probably want to, too."

He nodded. "But I'll see you tomorrow night," he said as if that cheered him up.

"You will," Neily assured him. "Early. So I can introduce you to your guests."

She hesitated, desperate to fill the silence. "Thanks for the pizza," she said then.

"Anytime," he said as if he meant it. He tapped the top frame of her car door before he stepped back and put an end to any idea of a good-night kiss.

And with that possibility snatched away, Neily got behind the wheel.

For some reason she remembered Miss Sela just then and called to Wyatt, "Thanks for the help with Miss Sela, too. I don't think I could have gotten her back to the hospital without you."

"Glad to be of service," he called in return as he unlocked his driver's-side door.

He didn't get into his car, though. He stayed standing there, watching her over the roof with an expression she couldn't decipher.

But in Neily's mind as she closed her own door, started her engine and finally pulled away, Wyatt was wondering if he should have kissed her after all.

And wishing he had.

Just like she was.

Chapter Five

"Noah...Perry—right?" Wyatt said as he approached one of his dinner guests on Wednesday evening.

He'd met so many people that he was struggling to remember all their names. The preponderance of Perrys and Pratts had made it more complicated, and despite the fact that he'd tried to keep Neily's five brothers separate in his mind from the many Perry males he wasn't sure he had. "Or am I getting it wrong and you're one of Neily's brothers?"

"Nope, you were right the first time, I'm Noah Perry," the man confirmed. "And I'm *not* one of Neily's brothers. Or even a cousin or a blood relative. Although we are connected by marriage now—my brother Jared is married to her sister Mara, her brother

Cam is married to my cousin Eden, and in a couple of days my other cousin Faith will marry Neily's other brother Boone."

As he'd listed them, Noah had pointed to the people themselves—all of whom had apparently volunteered on Sunday and were there tonight for the buffet supper that was intended to thank them.

Wyatt laughed. "In other words, there aren't just a lot of Perrys and Pratts, there's also a lot of *getting together* of the Perrys and the Pratts to make it even more confusing. Any other pairings in the wind?"

The minute Wyatt asked that he realized the question sounded weird. But it had just occurred to him that Neily could be involved with one of the Perrys herself. Noah even. And although he didn't understand why it was important to him, Wyatt really needed to know.

Fortunately Noah didn't seem to find the question too odd. "No, no other pairings that I know of. At the moment, anyway. But lately it's kind of hard to tell who might hook up next."

So Neily wasn't seeing a Perry. That didn't mean she wasn't seeing anyone else…

Not that it was any of his business. Or should matter to him even if she was.

And because he was trying to *make* it not matter to him, he abandoned that vein of conversation and went on to the reason he'd sought out Noah in the first place.

"Am I also remembering right and you're the local contractor?" Wyatt asked then.

"Yep."

"Okay, I'm batting two for two," he said, glad he wasn't mistaken. "I wanted to talk to you about doing some renovating and remodeling of this place."

Noah nodded, taking a swig of his beer. "It needs it."

"I know it'll be a big job. Is it something you could handle and—if it is—are you available?"

"I'll be between jobs after this week. What were you thinking about?"

Wyatt outlined everything from plumbing, electrical and insulating upgrades to window replacement, stripping wallpaper, repainting, and redoing the flooring in every room.

"So you're talking a complete fix-up," Noah summarized when he was finished.

"Pretty much. Is it within what you can do or will I need outside help?" Wyatt asked.

"I've built houses from the ground up around here. My crew and I can do whatever it takes."

"Of course Home-Max will supply all the materials but the labor would be up to you," Wyatt added.

Noah nodded again. "I haven't dealt with Home-Max much, but I liked what I saw at the Hardware Expo last month."

"You were there?"

"I was. And Home-Max impressed me. I'm generally stuck using what I can get around here—"

"From Hector Tyson's lumberyard—I just heard about him."

"Right. Home-Max offers a whole lot more options and innovative things I've never even worked with—especially when it comes to insulation. Hector isn't good about keeping up with changes. I'd like the chance to try out some of what I saw demo'd at the Expo."

"Great! Then why don't you come by as soon as you get the chance, and we'll go through room by room to give you a clear picture of what'll have to be done. Then you can work up a bid."

"Sounds good." Noah took another drink of his beer. "Does this mean you'll be staying on here?" he asked then.

"I'm not sure what will happen," Wyatt said, catching sight of Neily talking with a group of people.

She looked terrific tonight, with her shiny hair falling free around that porcelain-perfect face that he didn't seem to be able to get out of his mind. She was dressed in a pair of dark-gray slacks that hugged her backside so well he would have had to be blind not to notice. And on top she was wearing a see-through white blouse that allowed him to see the white T-shirt she wore underneath—but it was enough to drive him a little nuts anyway.

She seemed to be in her element with these people— she was smiling and laughing, her metallic blue eyes were glistening, and his own gaze just kept seeking her out while he wondered when he could find another excuse to join her….

But he was talking to Noah Perry now, he reminded himself. About the reason for the renovation and if it indicated that he'd be staying in Northbridge…

"Things are up in the air now. To some degree, where

we go from here will be up to Neily, as my grand-mother's social worker," Wyatt told his guest.

"You don't have to worry about Neily. She's great," Noah said. "We grew up together. Went to school together."

Too late—Wyatt was already worried about what she was bringing to life in him. " So she isn't too tough on the families she investigates?"

"She is when she has to be," Noah answered. "But I've never known her not to be fair."

This time Wyatt nodded. "Is she seeing anyone?"

Oh, man, where had that come from?

"I haven't heard that she is. Why? Are you interested?"

"Curious," Wyatt said in a hurry, still unable to believe that he'd actually ventured into this territory at all, let alone with someone who was a stranger to him and a friend of Neily's. "She just seems like someone who would have 'em lined up."

"Neily?" Noah repeated as if he took for granted what struck Wyatt as something special. "Neily's just Neily. She's great but…"

Out of the corner of his eye Wyatt saw him shrug.

"…I guess she's just Neily to me," Noah finished. "Somebody I've known forever. Like my sisters."

Wyatt finally managed to pull his gaze away from her before it got too obvious that he couldn't. It was just in time to see his guest finish his beer.

"Let me get you another one of those," he offered, not waiting for Noah to agree or disagree before he headed for the kitchen.

Passing Neily along the way, he caught a whiff of the faint, rainwater-scented perfume she was wearing tonight and he had to fight to keep himself from burying his nose in the side of her neck—that was how much he liked it.

But then he liked so much about her.

So much it was really rattling him. He'd actually felt like kissing her the night before. A woman who wasn't Mikayla.

He hadn't thought that would ever happen to him again and yet there he'd been, itching to do it.

And having to remind himself that he couldn't kiss the social worker who was judging whether or not he was a fit guardian for his grandmother. Even if he was willing to put himself out there like that again, which he wasn't.

How damn dumb was he, anyway? he'd been asking himself ever since.

He'd better not be dumb enough to kiss the social worker who couldn't possibly see him as anything but one of her cases.

But he *hadn't* kissed her, so at least that line hadn't been crossed and he'd spared himself from an embarrassing situation that would have caused her to tell him he *had* crossed the line.

A line that wasn't safe for him to cross even if he and Neily weren't in the positions they were in.

And that was something else he'd spent all night and all day today forcing himself to keep in mind.

Because what was coming awake in him were things that mirrored his early feelings for Mikayla and that left him thinking that if he *did* get into anything with Neily, it wouldn't be merely a meaningless fling. It could become something as serious for him as what he'd had with Mikayla.

And he just didn't want that. He couldn't risk it.

So he'd decided that if what it took was reminding himself of how bad it had been for him after Mikayla's death to keep avoiding the good he felt every time he was with Neily, that was what he was going to do.

Because a reminder of the pain was fleeting, but it still wasn't the real deal.

And the real deal was so much worse it was worth anything to stay away from.

"You wash and I'll dry," Neily said when she found Wyatt in the kitchen late Wednesday night.

"Thanks, but Mary Pat—"

"Went to bed. She was getting a migraine and I told her I'd fill in for her," Neily explained.

Staying after everyone else had left the dinner party had not been her intention. In fact, she'd planned to leave when everyone else did to *avoid* being alone with Wyatt and ending up in another good-night scene that could plant thoughts of kissing in her head again.

Which was why, as the party had begun to wind down, Neily had gone upstairs to see Theresa. But the visit that Neily had thought would be brief had instead stretched to accommodate Theresa's need to hear all the details of what was going on downstairs, despite the elderly woman's refusal to attend.

Then, when Neily had finally reached the end of

Theresa's questions, she'd happened across an obviously ill Mary Pat determined to go downstairs and help Wyatt clean. And like a glutton for punishment, Neily had assured the other woman that she would stand in for her.

So there she was, alone with Wyatt after all.

But only, she swore to herself, to do a few dishes before she bid him the quickest good-night in history.

"I can take care of everything myself if Mary Pat's sick," Wyatt said.

Neily shook her head. "It'll be faster and easier with two of us. And since your sleeves are already rolled up, you wash and I'll dry," she repeated.

"Thanks," he said without any more of a fight.

His rolled sleeves were on the sky-blue dress shirt he was wearing with a pair of khaki slacks. She couldn't help noticing how fabulous his rear end looked in the pants or how thick and sexy his bare forearms and wrists were.

"Nice party," she said to get her mind off both.

"I hope so. At home I would have tried to have something a little splashier, but there are a lot of limitations to a place that hasn't been occupied in decades."

"We're not fancy around here," Neily assured him, accepting the first of many plates to dry with the towel she'd found on the counter.

"Not fancy but close—everybody seems to know everybody—"

"That's how small towns are."

"Yeah, I wondered about that when we were driving here—whether it would be a picturesque small town or something more along the lines of a backwater full of

feuds and inbreeding. So far it seems like the picturesque version. Or is the feuding and inbreeding going
on behind the scenes?"

Neily laughed. "Well, maybe the feuding but the inbreeding is right out in the open," she joked. "No, really,
we're just a small college town that sprouted up from a
rural community. We're pretty much a what-you-see-is-
what-you-get kind of place."

"What I *saw* tonight was a whole lot of Pratts," Wyatt
said then. "There are seven of you?"

"Eight, actually. You also met Karis Walker tonight—
she's married to Luke Walker and she's our half sister."

"Different moms or dads?"

"Moms. Our father took off when we were just kids
and had a second family. There were two daughters
from that branch—one who died and Karis, who
brought our half niece back here and ended up with
Luke Walker."

"Your father *took off?*" Wyatt repeated, sounding genuinely bothered by the idea. "That must have been rough."

"It was rough on my mother. To be honest, I was too
young to remember him or a time when he was around.
He left right after Boone, Taylor and Jon were born—
just before I turned three."

"They were born at the same time?"

"That's what triplets do."

Wyatt smiled wryly at that. "I didn't know they
were triplets."

"Sorry, didn't I tell you that when I introduced them?
I usually do."

"I would definitely have remembered it if you had—I'm a triplet."

Neily looked from the platter she was drying to him. "You are?"

"Marti, Ry and I."

"Wow. I didn't know. And triplets are so rare—what are the odds?"

"Uh-oh. Triplets are more rare than twins but if a multiple birth happens, the chances of it happening again in the same family or later generations are higher. Maybe we're related," Wyatt said, grinning.

"I know all about my own family's history and it isn't even remotely connected to yours," Neily said with a laugh, thinking how easy it was to be with him…

Skittering away from that thought, she said, "But with triplets in my family and you *being* a triplet, we better never have kids together—they'll all come in threes."

But the notion of having babies with Wyatt was too tantalizing and that was even worse than thinking about how much she liked being with him.

Wyatt didn't respond to her comment, though. Instead he said, "I met a lot of Perrys tonight, too. Another big family?"

"Not the way we are, no. Eden, Eve and Faith are cousins to Jared, Noah, Kate and Meg."

"Ah, what little I know I got from Noah tonight but he didn't tell me that. He *did* tell me that a lot of the Perrys are married to or about to marry Pratts."

"True," she said.

"But not you."

"No..." Neily said tentatively. She wasn't sure what Wyatt was getting at.

"What about someone else? There's no wedding ring and you've never mentioned a husband, so I figured you're single, but it just struck me tonight that between shopping Monday night, pizza last night and now tonight—I've been keeping you from whoever you're involved with...*if* you're involved with someone."

Was he trying to find out if she had a man in her life?

Neily couldn't help smiling from ear to ear and she didn't want him to see it—even though he was steadfastly looking into the sink rather than at her. She turned her back to him to set the platter on the kitchen table, buying herself a minute to consider her answer.

Their other conversations had revolved around jobs or Theresa and the mystery that surrounded her—surface subjects that were perfectly appropriate for them to discuss. But this was personal.

And that left her with a choice—to allow it, or to tell him she didn't discuss her personal life with someone who was involved with one of her cases.

But if she allowed it, she might get a little information about *his* personal life. Information she was curious about but that wasn't really any of her business because it didn't pertain to his grandmother...

"You're not keeping me from anyone because there *isn't* anyone at the moment," she said, deciding suddenly to go ahead and take that fork in the road. Clearly her desires were outweighing her better judgment.

She returned to the spot beside the sink to take the last dish to dry as Wyatt drained the water. Then he grabbed a second towel and turned to face her, leaning his hips against the counter's edge to look at her.

And while his expression didn't show much surprise at the information that she was single and free, it did seem as if he was trying to hide the fact that he was glad to hear it.

But now it was her turn.

"What about you? Did you leave someone special home alone in Missoula to come here?"

He was still smiling, but sadness veiled his eyes. "No." He glanced down at the dish towel in his hands, toying with the cloth. "I was married but she died."

Mikayla and the baby—that first night when Wyatt and Mary Pat had arrived, when Theresa had asked him about Mikayla and the baby, he'd gently reminded his grandmother that they'd died...

"Was that Mikayla?" Neily asked. "Theresa mistook me for her again tonight."

"Yeah, Mikayla was my wife," Wyatt answered. "I told you that first night we met."

"No, you said I looked a little familiar. I guessed it was to someone named Mikayla because your grandmother had been mistaking me for her. But you didn't explain *who* Mikayla was."

Or anything about the baby...

Could she ask about that now? Somehow it didn't feel like the right time so she merely said, "I'm sorry."

He raised his eyebrows in a helpless shrug. "Life

hands you a bowl of fruit—some of it's ripe, some of it's rotten."

She hesitated to go any further because she had the sense that he didn't want to say more. Especially since he suddenly seemed remote as he dried his hands and those forearms of his in a slow motion that had an innate sensuality to it and made Neily's mouth go dry to watch.

Then he pushed away from the counter with his hips, tossed aside the dishrag, and said, "It's a work night for you and here I am keeping you again."

Neily couldn't be sure if he was being considerate or if he wanted her to go rather than talk more about his late wife. Either way, she set down her towel, too, and said, "I *should* head home. I have to see Miss Sela at the crack of dawn tomorrow and check her out of the hospital if she's ready to be released."

"But we'll still be seeing you tomorrow, too, right?" Wyatt said as he walked her to the door. He sounded hopeful enough for her to dispel the thought that he was trying to get rid of her now.

"You will," she assured him. "Theresa and I are having tea."

They'd reached the front door and Wyatt retrieved her jacket from a closet nearby. As he did, he said, "I also understand that there's a big basketball game tomorrow night."

"I don't know if I'd call it a *big* basketball game," Neily said. "The local guys get together to play each other. They call themselves the Bruisers and play whatever sport is in season, so right now it's basketball. The games aren't for anything but fun, but they do usually draw a crowd—small towns are short on entertainment, and we have to keep down the inbreeding somehow."

Wyatt was facing her again and that made him grin in that way he had that she just found so, so sexy...

"I thought I might go," he announced then. "Are you interested or is it something you don't like?"

"No, I go to them all," she said in a hurry. Too much of a hurry to conceal the flash of excitement that had gone through her at the invitation.

"It seems pretty innocent—I mean, it should be okay for the social worker to go to a local basketball game with someone under her microscope, shouldn't it?"

Neily considered that the way she'd considered whether or not to allow the exchange of personal information. Now, knowing for sure that he was a widower, that somewhere in his past there was a woman he'd adored and lost, Neily had a second reason not to get involved with him. A reason from her own past that warned her away from anyone who might have any kind of expectations of the perfect woman for her to compete with.

And yet...

A basketball game *was* pretty innocent. And she *did* still need to get to know him for Theresa's sake...

"I think it's okay," she said, albeit tentatively.

"Something for me to look forward to, then," he said quietly.

He held her coat open and Neily slipped into it before returning to face him. When she did, they were much closer together. And standing like that, at the door, to say good-night, once again put thoughts of kissing into her head.

The quickest good-night in history, she reminded herself.

Yet she just stood there, gazing up into that face she'd dreamed about every night since she'd met him.

He was looking down at her intently, his eyes searching hers, and she had the sense that he was torn. She'd been convinced the night before that he'd been considering kissing her and she just knew it was on his mind again.

But don't let him, she warned herself.

Wyatt shook his head and she thought it must be in denial of his own impulses, that he wasn't going to kiss her.

But she was wrong.

Because just then he leaned forward enough to barely touch his lips to hers.

It was only a scant whisper of a kiss. Over in a split second. Then he straightened and grimaced slightly, screwing up those handsome features with a look of wry devilishness.

"I know," he said before she could say anything. "I shouldn't have done that. I just—" He shook his head. "I just had to do it anyway."

The same way she'd had to let him…

But, no, he shouldn't have. So that was what she addressed. "We wouldn't want anyone thinking I wasn't impartial because—"

"My fault. I take full responsibility. Shoot me."

She couldn't help smiling at his over-the-top challenge. "We don't have to go that far—"

"Just don't do it again," he finished.

Which was, in fact, what she'd been about to say. And yet when he did, something inside of her sank at the prospect.

Still, she agreed and reiterated, "I need to be impartial."

"And you think *that* kiss was good enough to sway you?" he joked.

He didn't wait for an answer, though, his eyes still holding hers as he opened the front door. "Tomorrow I'll be the model of good behavior, I promise."

Neily mimicked his nod to confirm that that would be for the best. But she didn't say anything except goodnight before she left.

Because although she might know the model of good behavior was what they *both* should be from here on, deep down she just couldn't make herself root for it.

Chapter Six

It was midafternoon Thursday when Neily got to her office and found a message that Cheryl Abrams had called. Ordinarily Neily worked under the supervision of a man in Billings. But because Theresa had come from Missoula and her case was being handled there, the supervisor Neily reported to was Cheryl. She had been Neily's supervisor from Billings for two years before moving, so Neily knew her well.

"Hi, this is Neily Pratt. I'm returning Cheryl's phone call..."

"Hey, Neily, how're tricks?" was Cheryl's greeting when she got on the line.

They exchanged small talk for a few minutes before Cheryl got down to business.

"The Grayson case," she said. "I have the report from this end sitting in front of me. I wanted to know where things stand at your end."

Neily outlined her evaluation of Theresa, agreeing with prior medical and psychological tests.

"It's amazing that she had the oomph to take the keys and get here," Neily said. "I can only assume that she had a spurt of determination so strong that it temporarily over-shadowed everything else and allowed her to pull this off."

"What about that get-back-what-was-taken-from-her thing?" Cheryl asked, obviously reading it from something in front of her.

"That's what caused the determination to get here and she's still saying it. But now that she's here, her other issues have taken precedence again, and she's fearful and confused. She won't—or can't—explain it, hasn't done anything else about it, and no one can figure out what it might mean. Or if it's just a product of her delusions—which is possible. Have you guys come across anything that might have been taken from her—has anyone men-tioned that she's missing money, jewelry, anything?"

"We've been asking but, no, nothing like that. The housekeeper assumed we were thinking one of the grandkids could have stolen from Theresa and she defended them like a dog protecting her pups. She says that the grandkids make sure Theresa has everything she ever shows an interest in, and that Theresa is generally too lost in her own world to even realize what's at her disposal, let alone care. Plus the granddaughter, Marti, volunteered to take our social worker through Theresa's room—everything of value matched what's on the list the insurance company provided."

"Well, I do get the feeling that whatever it is that Theresa thinks was taken from her is bigger and more important than money or jewelry or something like that."

"How about her physical exam—you had her checked there, right?"

"First thing. She got a medical stamp of approval— no indications of any kind of abuse or neglect. From what I've seen, her grandson and her caregiver treat her like she's made of glass."

"What *about* the grandson and the caregiver? What do they have to say about each other?"

"Rave reviews on both sides. And for both of them from Theresa. Theresa is actually calmed by having either of them near her—there's no fear, no holding back, nothing that gives me any suspicion that she's abused by or afraid of either of them."

"We've gotten the same picture here. Like I said, there's a housekeeper—she lives in with her husband, who does gardening services. They both speak highly of the current nurse's and the grandchildren's treatment of Theresa. There was another nurse before the one employed in that capacity now. We tracked her down, talked to her. She only left because she wanted to retire, and she says that in all the years she worked with Theresa she never saw signs of anything remotely suspicious. She's impressed—and a little jealous, it sounds like—of how devoted the three grandchildren are to Theresa. Neighbors, friends, some people in the workplace—all the same."

Neily was relieved to hear what Cheryl was saying. It let her know that she hadn't somehow missed something because of her attraction to Wyatt.

"What about the other two grandchildren?" Neily asked, more out of her own curiosity about Wyatt's siblings than anything. "Tempers? Resentments toward Theresa or having to work the family business? Anything along those lines?"

"No indications of any of that. From all reports, they're a close family, they get along, like each other, work well together, and share the care of Theresa evenly enough that no one feels overburdened or resentful. What about your guy?"

Her guy...

Neily was trying *not* to think of him in those terms.

"Same. He's down-to-earth, endlessly patient, calm, understanding, intelligent, has a good sense of humor—" She stopped herself, realizing not all of that was what mattered as the guardian of his grandmother, that some of it was what she'd been cataloging as the assets of the man himself. "He's great with Theresa—caring, compassionate, kind—" All of which Neily also found attractive...

But she cut to the chase before she got carried away with accolades for Wyatt. "I don't have the impression that he sees Theresa as a burden, either."

"Looks like we should all be lucky enough to have

these people taking care of us if we needed it, huh?" Cheryl said.

"Looks like it," Neily agreed, again reassured that she wasn't the only one coming to that conclusion.

"So from this end," Cheryl was saying into Neily's wandering thoughts, "there's no indication that Theresa was escaping a bad situation. You'd agree with that?"

"I would. I think this was prompted either by Theresa's mental and emotional problems, or by something so far back in her past that not even her grandchildren have any idea what it might be."

"And clearly she's unable to live on her own, but her family is making sure she doesn't have to."

"Right."

"It seems as if we're all on the same page," Cheryl said, drawing this to an end. "I have a class reunion in Billings this weekend, so Saturday—before I go to that—I'll come into Northbridge to do one home visit of my own just to put my formal stamp of approval on this. You can give me your written report then, but I'd say that there's no reason to believe that there's anything wrong with this family or with the care they're providing. I'll leave it to you to visit with Theresa occasionally from here on if they stay in Northbridge—just to touch base and make sure any services that might benefit her are available. But on the whole, I'd say we can recommend that she remain in the family's care and call it a day on this one."

"Great," Neily said.

The conversation went from professional to personal

again for a few more minutes before they said goodbye. And that was when Neily sat back in her desk chair and truly felt a weight lifted off her shoulders.

She hadn't really thought that her own judgment of Theresa's situation was being colored by whatever it was that seemed to be drawing her to Wyatt, but she hadn't been sure. At least now she could rest assured that she wasn't the only one finding nothing questionable about Theresa's care or her caregivers, so it was unlikely that she'd missed anything.

Thank goodness. She breathed out a long sigh. Now she was, for the most part, free of *that* worry. Free to explore the attraction to Wyatt.

Oh, no...

She hadn't really just thought that, had she? Because that was *not* a good idea. Even if he wasn't under her investigation any longer, it wasn't as if all signs pointed to go.

The fact that Wyatt was a widower still did—and should—give her pause, she told herself.

What she was looking for in a relationship was a clear path, not one shadowed by expectations she couldn't live up to—she'd already been on that road in her last relationship and it was rocky and had led to a dead end. And while she might be mistaken, it seemed to her that there couldn't be anything bigger to live up to than the ghost of a late wife.

Add to that the resemblance she apparently had to that late wife, and that only seemed to Neily to make it worse. To make it more likely that either consciously or subconsciously Wyatt could be hoping that there would be more similarities that could make her a replacement for a person he'd loved and lost.

So, no, she told herself. She was *not* going to allow herself the freedom to explore her attraction to Wyatt.

She was free to help him with Theresa. She was free to be friends with him, even to go to the basketball game with him tonight—just to be neighborly. But that was it. She was absolutely *not* free to do anything else.

The fact that she hadn't overlooked something that could have harmed Theresa meant that she'd dodged a bullet professionally, and now there was no way she was going to let things with Wyatt go any further and risk that she wasn't so lucky personally.

Certainly she hadn't been in the past, and she'd learned from experience.

She breathed another sigh of relief to have made up her mind.

It seemed so clear. So straightforward. And at that moment she felt completely on top of it all. She knew what she wanted, what she didn't want, and a widower was in the didn't-want column. Cut and dry. No problem.

Except kissing him last night—and dying to kiss him again so much it made her ache—proved she wasn't exactly on top of it all.

Or maybe on top of any of it...

Chapter Seven

"I learned something interesting from your grand-mother today," Neily told Wyatt as they settled into the bleachers at the high-school gymnasium Thursday evening to wait for the basketball game to begin.

"Interesting and believable, or interesting and questionable?" Wyatt asked.

"Believable, I think," Neily said. "She mistook me for Mikayla again and when I told her who I was, she looked at me as if it had just dawned on her. She said she knew my grandparents—on my father's side. That she and my grandmother were close friends when they were both girls."

"Any chance your grandmother is still living and could give us some information?" Wyatt asked.

"She's still living—in northern Wyoming—and I'll definitely ask her. She's been on a cruise and she doesn't get back until Saturday. I'm making the three-hour drive to Sheridan on Sunday to have lunch with her."

"Your grandmother never mentioned mine?" Wyatt asked.

"Not in any way that I recall," Neily answered. "She's talked about when she was young, about things she and her friends did, but if she ever said anything specifically about Theresa it didn't stick out in my mind."

Still more people filtered into the gym and again there was a pause to say hello.

Then Wyatt said, "Hector Tyson is out of town, too. He isn't out of town with your grandmother, is he?"

"How do you know he's away?" Neily asked in surprise.

"I looked him up this afternoon—that's where I was when you came for your visit with Gram. I went to Tyson's house to see if I could talk to him. But he's—"

"In Denver," Neily supplied. "I could have saved you the trip. He goes every year at this time for a checkup at National Jewish Hospital. It has a respiratory center—he has emphysema."

"See how much it helps to have the inside line? All I found out was that he wasn't around."

"And he won't be for a while. He always stays in Denver longer than his exam takes. It's his getaway, he says."

"So we won't be able to talk to him any time soon?"

We again. It really, really shouldn't have delighted her as much as it did...

"Not until he comes back, and when that will be is anybody's guess," Neily said. "Some years he stays a couple of weeks, some years longer. It's an open-ended kind of thing."

The game started then and that was where their attention became focused. Wyatt had no problem getting into the spirit of it along with the rest of the onlookers. He stood up and cheered with everyone when crucial baskets were made; he groaned when penalties and fouls were called.

Neily actually thought it was more entertaining to watch him than the game. And not only because he looked amazing in a navy-blue crewneck sweater that showed off a strong, thick neck, and jeans that outlined his muscular legs. She added his enthusiasm, his lack of shyness, and his ability to fit in to the things she liked about him.

If only she could have found something she *didn't* like about him. But even though she tried to balance the scale with something on the negative side, she couldn't find a single thing.

When the game ended Neily and Wyatt filed out of the gym with everyone else. But once they were in the corridor Wyatt nodded in the direction opposite the exit and said, "So is this where you went to school?"

"Yes, high school. The other two buildings on the compound are for elementary school and middle school—that's where I went for those grades."

"Show me around?" he said as if he were enticing her into something rather than making a request.

She wasn't sure why he wanted a tour, but she wasn't in any hurry for the evening to end so she opted to comply.

"Well, you've already seen the gym, the locker rooms are there—"

"Show me where you had classes."

"Okay…" she said, as if she were humoring a request that didn't altogether make sense. They began to walk deeper into the building. "Well, I *did* take gym. I burned muffins in the home-ec room over there and did bad collages in art class," she narrated as they passed each room. "I didn't take auto repair or technical arts—those were more the boy classes."

"So you weren't a tomboy? Even with five brothers?"

"No, I wouldn't say I was ever a tomboy."

"What would you say you were?" he asked as they wandered through the quiet halls.

"When I was here I was…" How should she put it without sounding bad? "A hell-raiser?"

That made him laugh. "You?" he said as if it was too far-fetched to believe.

They'd reached the front of the building where the office that served all three levels of academia was housed. Neily nodded at the sign on the door of the principal's office. "I spent more than my fair share of time in there."

"For what?" he challenged. "Helping little old ladies across the street when you were supposed to be in class?"

"Again with the little old ladies? Sorry to disappoint you, but I'm telling you, I gave my poor mother some gray hair."

She didn't know why that seemed to amuse him so much, but when she glanced at him she found him grinning as big as she had the night before, when she'd realized he was fishing for information about her love life.

"Neily-Pratt-Social-Worker was a bad girl?" he said.

"Not *bad* bad," she qualified. "I didn't mug little old ladies or vandalize property or break into houses— actually, I was part of a group who broke into your house once for a party, but—"

"You broke into Gram's house to party?"

"Once. It's happened here and there over the years— an old vacant house just sitting there is an invitation for kids to get into mischief."

"No wonder there was so much to clean. Here I thought you guys were all being nice, and you were really just coming in and cleaning up the messes you made partying there," he joked.

"There was probably some of that in everybody's mind," she admitted with a laugh.

She showed him more classrooms and told him stories of the insurrection she'd incited in Spanish, and various other tales of the trouble she'd gotten into.

They headed back the way they'd come then, finally leaving the school just as the Bruisers were coming out of the locker room after showering.

The team encouraged them to go to Adz—the popular pub and restaurant where everyone went postgame.

"That would mean a lot of talking to other people, though," Wyatt said out of the team's hearing. "How about I buy you an ice cream cone for the walk back to the house instead?"

Because then it would just be the two of them. That was the unspoken part of that invitation and what Neily knew she should avoid. And yet she heard herself agree anyway.

As they crossed the combination playground and sports field to South Street and headed for the ice cream parlor, Wyatt said, "Okay, now tell me what made you a hell-raiser outside of school."

"Ah, well, that would have been the climbing out my bedroom window to meet my friends after curfew, and getting caught driving a car before I had a license. And once I made a call on a stolen cell phone—but in my defense, I didn't know the phone was stolen, and I *was* calling home to check in, the way I was supposed to."

"You *were* a bad kid," Wyatt judged, but with a smile to let her know he was entertained by the notion as they reached the ice cream shop.

He paid for their cones, and after they finished, they'd helped themselves to the peppermint candies at the ice cream shop's door before they resumed their walk back to the Hobbs house.

After unwrapping the candies and popping them into their mouths, Neily picked up their earlier conversation where they'd left off.

"What about you?" she asked. "Were you Mr. Clean growing up?"

His smile was too mischievous to be a denial. "There were a few minor infractions, but I never used a stolen cell phone," he said as if that were the worst possible crime.

"I knew it—Mr. Clean," she accused.

He didn't take the bait and give her any details of a misspent youth, he merely went on smiling. "What about boyfriends? Did you have a lot of those?"

Her love life again. He did seem to have an inordinate interest in that…

"Tonight is all about me, is that it?" she asked.

"Come on, satisfy my curiosity," he urged.

And he was just so hard to refuse. Besides, once again she was enjoying herself.

"Boyfriends," she repeated "Yes, I had my share of those. I went to all the dances—one of them in a dress so short they sent me home."

"I would like to have seen *that!*" he said, giving her a lascivious glance. Then he said, "First kiss."

"Hmm… The *first* first kiss was when I was eleven and I kissed the boy on a dare—it was the beginning of my notorious youth."

"But dares don't count. I'm talking about the first real kiss."

"That was at your house."

"Last night? I gave you your first kiss?" he joked.

"No, not last night," she answered, although she had to admit that even that almost-nothing kiss of the previous evening had stayed with her longer than the other kiss she'd had at the Hobbs house. "At the party we had when we broke into your grandmother's house."

He laughed. "Seriously?"

"Seriously. Just before the police came in and made us all leave—it was supposed to have been a make-out party," she confided.

"And I missed it—that doesn't seem fair," he said.

"What about your first kiss? And don't do that mystery-man thing again," she warned.

Neily gave him a sidelong glance to go with her warning, and she caught sight of his profile in the moonlight. The man was just too handsome, she decided when she had to drag her eyes off him.

"My first kiss..." he said. "That would have been when I was ten. I had an intense crush on the babysitter, saw my opportunity when she was helping me with my homework and I took it!"

"That's more like the dare than the first kiss," Neily decided. "I had to tell you about *my* first real kiss, now you tell me about yours."

"The first tip-my-head, close-my-eyes, part-my-lips kiss?"

Those details just made her remember the kiss *they'd* shared. And die for it all over again...

"That first kiss was with Chrissy Whitman," he said, finally complying. "I was fourteen, she was sixteen and had no idea just how much of a rookie I was because I pretended that I really got around. I took her by the shoulders, tipped my head, closed my eyes, parted my lips, moved in..." he grinned "...and missed."

Neily laughed, which helped lessen some of her own increasing craving for just what he was describing. "And missed?"

"Apparently I should have waited to close my eyes until a little later in the transaction. As it was I missed the lips completely, skidded off her chin and fell face-first into her neck. It wasn't pretty."

"It also doesn't count as a first kiss since you missed," Neily pointed out in the midst of laughing at him.

His answering smile was devilish. "I told you, Chrissy had it bad for me. She recovered, took the blame and on the next try I'd learned my lesson—eyes open until contact! From there Chrissy became the source of a few more firsts…"

And Neily ended up jealous of someone named Chrissy Whitman from far back in Wyatt's past…

To hide it, she goaded him. "So what you're saying is that you've always had a thing for older women."

He shrugged a negligent, cocky shoulder. "There's something to be said for experience."

Neily laughed again.

They'd reached his house by then and she went to her car. She opened the driver's-side door and stepped into the lee of it to put it between herself and Wyatt.

"I won't be seeing Theresa tomorrow," she said then. She hadn't told him anything that she'd discussed with her supervisor so he didn't know yet that he and his family had passed inspection. "It's my brother Boone's wedding day," she continued. "I'm part of the wedding party and I have a million last-minute things to do—"

"I know, he invited me."

Neily hadn't forgotten. In fact she'd been fantasizing about what Wyatt was going to look like in a suit.

Still, she pretended his invitation had slipped her mind because she didn't want him to know that the possibility of him coming had made her all the more eager for the event. "That's right, he did invite you, didn't he? At your thank-you dinner. You and Mary Pat and Theresa, too."

"Yeah. I'm working on Gram, but odds are against her going."

"You'll be there, though, won't you?" Too hopeful. Neily wanted to kick herself.

"I'd planned on it. I even bought a gift while I was out today. Luckily I brought dress clothes with me in case I had to do some kind of court appearance or something for Gram once I was here."

"I guess I'll see you tomorrow night, then," Neily said, ordering herself to get in the car so she was out of range of anything like what had happened the night before.

And yet she stayed where she was...

"I guess I'll see you tomorrow night, too," he said, his eyes focused on hers, his expression unreadable.

"You know," he said after a moment, in a deep, quiet voice, "when I'm not with you I know how this should go and I'm sure I can be that model of good behavior I told you I would be. But then I spend a little time with you and..."

"And?" she asked just as softly when he stalled.

"And I can't not do this..." he said. One hand came up to the side of her face, and he demonstrated what he'd outlined for her as his technique—tipping his head, parting his lips, leaning forward to press his mouth to hers just before his eyes closed.

Then Neily's eyes closed, too, and she surrendered to the defeat of some intentions of her own, kissing him back.

Only unlike the kiss of the previous evening, this wasn't so quick. It wasn't so much the kind he'd probably given his babysitter, or the kind she'd given on a dare, either. Tonight he stayed and made it a real kiss. His lips parted, enticing hers to part, too. His head swayed the slightest bit, expertly soothing, lulling, and at the same time, drawing her deeper into that kiss that mingled his minty breath with hers as his hand cupped her jawline and held her there.

And yet, when this one was over, it still didn't seem like enough....

Neily opened her eyes to find him looking down into hers again.

"I don't know what it is..." he said more to himself than to her. "But I guess I can't behave with you."

He leaned in and kissed her again—short and sweet this time—and then he stepped back, obviously waiting for her to get into her car.

Which she did.

Then he closed her door and took another step back so she could pull away from the curb once she'd started her engine.

And all the while she couldn't really think about anything but that kiss and how much she wished they *were* just kids who could have been parked somewhere, making out like crazy.

And like him, she didn't know what it was about the time they spent together that made it so impossible to behave herself.

Chapter Eight

"Hey, Grams…" Wyatt said quietly from the door of the sunroom early Friday evening. He didn't want to startle Theresa, who was sitting where she did much of the time—staring out the rear windows where she could look down at Northbridge.

His grandmother raised a dazed expression to him but perked up when his presence registered.

"Oh, don't you look handsome! Like a movie star!" she said dotingly.

Wyatt smiled at her compliment and went to stand near her chair.

"What's the occasion?" Theresa asked, taking his hand and laying her cheek to the back of it for a moment before letting it go.

"Neily's brother is getting married," he said as if they hadn't talked about it already—this morning at breakfast and again at lunch. "You and Mary Pat were invited, too. Are you sure you don't want to come?"

"I can't, Wyatt. I can't," she lamented.

"I'd stay right with you every minute," he promised. "It might be nice for you to get out, maybe see some old friends…"

At breakfast his grandmother had merely wandered out of the room when he'd suggested that. At lunch she'd smiled vacantly and turned to ask Mary Pat for more mustard on her sandwich. But tonight his cajoling was met with a look of panic that he hadn't intended to cause.

"No," his grandmother said. "I can't face people. I'm too ashamed."

That was the first time he'd heard anything about shame.

"What are you ashamed of?" he asked gently.

But rather than an answer Theresa shook her head wildly and said, "I'm sorry for what I did, Wyatt. I should never have done it! Never! But I did and now I can't look people in the eye."

"Is this about selling the land to Hector Tyson?" he asked, confused.

"Hector Tyson," Theresa said with contempt.

Wyatt had told her after meeting Miss Sela that he'd heard about Hector Tyson buying the land. But every mention of that name had elicited the same response without any explanation.

"I told you that we know you're right," he went on.

"That you *did* own the land and that you did sell it to Hector Tyson. There's nothing for you to be embarrassed about in that."

His grandmother merely shook her head again.

Wyatt hunkered down in front of her, taking her hands in his this time. "I want to help you, Gram. You know I'll do anything I can for you. But you need to give me a little something to work with. If it's the land that was taken from you, that you want returned, I can't do that because there are houses there now that people own and live in. But I can go after restitution if something was wrong with the deal you made to sell it."

Theresa did one final shake of her head and then just stared at him.

Wyatt decided to try a different angle. "You went to a lot of trouble to get here so you could get something back. But now that you're here, you just sit at this window or the window in your bedroom upstairs—how is that going to get you what you came for?"

"I'm looking," Theresa said as if it should have been obvious.

Wyatt stopped short. At home in Missoula Theresa spent a lot of time staring out of windows, too. It hadn't occurred to him that when she was doing the same thing here there was a reason for it.

"What are you looking for?"

She shook her head again and tears filled her eyes. "I can't say it."

"I'll help you look if you just tell me what you're looking for."

Theresa once more shook her head, clearly fighting the tears. Wyatt couldn't stand to see her upset so he patted her hand comfortingly and said, "It's okay. I just want to do whatever makes you feel better."

Theresa smiled a sad, hopeless smile and then, as if she had just noticed that he was wearing his good navy-blue suit, she said, "Why are you all dressed up?"

Sometimes she just broke his heart.

"I'm going to a wedding. Neily's brother is getting married tonight."

"I like Neily. She's good to me."

The fact that Theresa had remembered Neily this time was a minor step in the right direction.

"I like Neily, too," Wyatt confessed.

"I know you do," Theresa said as if she knew more than he realized. "I'm glad. Go and be with her. I'm fine."

Theresa was not fine but Wyatt knew there was nothing he could do about that so he brought her hand to his mouth and kissed the back of it before he released it.

"Mary Pat can reach me on my cell phone if you need anything or if you just want me to come home," he said.

"Don't worry. Mary Pat will take care of me."

Wyatt got to his feet, bent over his grandmother's chair and kissed her forehead. "Good night, Gram."

"Have a good time with Neily."

"Oh, I will," Wyatt said. As he left the sunroom he thought that he didn't have to be told to have a good time with Neily. It just happened whenever he was with her.

Which was why he couldn't seem to make himself stay away from her.

He paused at the cracked mirror hanging on the wall outside the sunroom to do one final check of the knot on his silver-gray tie. It needed a tug to make it straight under the collar of his pale-gray shirt. As he adjusted it, it occurred to him that every other time he'd been on his way to see Neily he'd lectured himself about who she was and how he didn't want to get involved with her or with anyone else who could put him through the heartache of loss again.

But tonight he didn't have to do that.

Because sometime after Neily had driven away last night, he'd realized that trying to resist his attraction to her was failing pretty miserably, and that he'd better come up with a plan that had more chance to succeed.

So he'd hashed through it all night, and what he'd come up with was a plan not to let down his guard completely, but to roll with whatever was happening between them. To wade in cautiously—*very* cautiously. And only into the shallow end.

He was hoping if he eased up slightly on himself, if he relaxed, if he stopped making Neily such forbidden fruit, it might be enough to take the edge off and actually leave him more able to weather this.

At least that was the plan—to be like a tree in the wind and bend a little so he didn't break.

He also had to keep in mind that his visit to Northbridge was only temporary. That even if his grandmother ended up wanting to stay, he and Marti and Ry would still live and work in Missoula, and just take turns coming here to see Gram and make sure she was being taken care of without actually moving here themselves.

Wyatt sighed. Bend so he didn't break for the time being until he could figure out how to distance himself from Neily and get on top of this hold she had on him.

Was it a great solution? he asked himself as he took his car keys out of his pocket and headed for the front door.

No, it wasn't. It was just the only one he could come up with.

Bend so he didn't break…

And if in the bending a few innocent kisses were exchanged?

It was tough even for him to see that as high-risk behavior.

As long as a little bending, a little kissing, was as far as it went.

Chapter Nine

"You're supposed to be a husband first and *then* become a proud papa."

"That doesn't count when the baby has four legs. Now let's get inside again before my bride thinks I've deserted her for a horse."

The wedding guests laughed and began to move away from the paddock with Boone when he headed back to his ranch house.

"I could still use a little air. How about we stay out here?" Wyatt whispered in Neily's ear.

"Okay," she answered. She'd had four glasses of champagne; when they'd followed her brother from his wedding reception out to his barn to see his new foal, she'd hoped the late-evening air would clear her head. It hadn't yet, so she was willing to give it more time.

And to steal a few minutes alone with Wyatt.

"So," he said when they were the only two left standing at the paddock rail, "A traditional ceremony with a barbecue reception. Marble cake. Black and white bridesmaid dresses—is there a yin-and-yang theme to this wedding, or am I imagining things?"

"You're not imagining things," Neily told him. "Yes, there is sort of a theme. Or an inside joke, maybe. In case you haven't noticed, Faith and Boone are about as opposite as two people can be. My brother is a rough-and-tumble kind of guy who wrangles and wrestles and cleans up after all sorts of animals both as the local vet and out here on his ranch. Faith is into art and culture and elegance and sophistication—she left Northbridge in search of the finer things of life. Then she came back here after her divorce. Them getting together is about the last matchup anyone would have predicted, but here they are."

"As different as black and white," Wyatt repeated. "Which, by the way, you look very nice in. I haven't had a chance to tell you," he said, glancing at her and at the bridesmaid dress she was wearing. It *was* black and white—a black sleeveless empire-waist dress over a white underlayer that reached just the tops of her knees.

"You clean up pretty well yourself," she countered. She was understating the truth because no fantasy of how he might look in a suit had done him justice.

Unfortunately her dress left her arms and shoulders bare, and the night air was chilly—especially with a storm threatening. And at that moment a shiver shook her without warning.

Wyatt saw it and took off his suit coat to drape around her shoulders.

"Thanks." She snuggled into it and breathed deeply the faint smell of his cologne. It made her wish for his arms around her instead....

"So why no date for your own brother's wedding?" Wyatt asked then, looking back at the foal and its mother.

Neily had actually forgotten that she *hadn't* had a date because Wyatt had filled that role so well. He had rarely left her side from the moment the ceremony had ended and the reception had begun. They'd discussed Theresa and the things his grandmother had said to him before he'd left home. Then they'd left that more serious conversation behind to simply chat with each other and with the other guests, to joke and tease and dance and celebrate the happy occasion.

Wyatt had been attentive and entertaining, and somehow along the way Neily had given up reminding herself that they weren't there as a real couple.

In answer to his question about being dateless she shrugged. "There was no one I wanted to bring," she said simply, because it was true. Or at least it had been until she'd met Wyatt. But under the circumstances it would have been inappropriate to ask him.

"I have to tell you, the more I get to know you, and looking at you tonight..." which he did again with a flattering appreciation in his eyes "...I just don't get it.

How is it that some guy hasn't snatched you up and put a ring on *your* finger?"

Maybe it was another effect of the champagne but this third probe into her love life only made her smile.

"First you wanted to know if you were keeping me from someone special. Last night you wanted to hear about my maiden voyages into kissing. Now you want to know about my marital history?" she said to give him a hard time, even though she already knew she was going to tell him what he wanted to know just so he'd stop fishing for the information.

"Yep." He cast her that smile of his that would have gotten just about anything he wanted out of her. "Have you ever been married?" he asked, taking a more direct approach this time as he turned to sling an arm along the top rail so he could now face her rather than the horses.

"No, I've never been married," Neily admitted. "I got close once but it didn't end up happening."

"Really?" he said. "Why did you kick the poor guy to the curb?"

Neily laughed. "Who says I was the one who called it off? Maybe he did."

Wyatt shook his head. "He'd have had to be crazy."

She didn't know if Wyatt was trying to be extra charming tonight or if his open flirting with her was just coming naturally, but she was still a sucker for it and laughed again.

"Well, actually," she said, "I think he *was* a little crazy, but you're right—it was me who called off the engagement."

"*You*—the social worker and counselor of people with emotional and mental problems—were with a guy who was crazy?"

"And you think the irony of that is funny?" Neily challenged him good-naturedly because he was so clearly enjoying that irony.

He sobered his so-handsome face. "Sorry. It *is* ironic, but I'm sure it wasn't funny."

"No, not at the time," she admitted. "And it probably isn't fair to say Trent was *crazy*. He was just wound a little too tight."

"Was he—*is* he—from around here?" Wyatt asked more seriously.

"No. He's a psychologist in Billings. I met him through work—one of his patients moved here and ended up on my caseload. I had to consult with him and we hit it off."

"A not-quite-crazy-but-wound-too-tight shrink?"

"I know, more irony."

"How long were you with him?"

"We dated long-distance for about a year before we got engaged, then I moved to Billings for the four months before we broke up and I came back here."

"So why the split?"

More interested in Wyatt than in the horses, Neily turned to face him, too, drinking in the sight of his sharply etched features in the light cast from a huge fixture above the barn doors. "I couldn't be what Trent wanted me to be," she answered.

"You couldn't be what he wanted you to be, so you broke up with *him?*"

"Right."

Wyatt's brows pulled together in just a flash of a confused frown. "How did that work?"

Some residual sadness came over Neily at the memories that sprang to mind. "It isn't easy to live up to what someone wants when that someone wants what you aren't. Initially Trent just seemed like a really together kind of guy—he got a lot accomplished because he was energetic without being hyper at all. He had a great, positive attitude. He was well-organized and efficient. He was—"

"Really together," Wyatt repeated as if he didn't want to hear any more of her accolades of the other man.

"He also seemed to know himself, what he wanted, where he was going in life. He had a clear view of things and I liked that."

"What *didn't* you like?"

Neily smiled at Wyatt's open quest to hear the negative.

"Part of what Trent had a clear view of was what the perfect woman was, what the perfect relationship should be, what the perfect life and marriage were. It was as if somewhere along the way he'd written a script for himself that he just *had* to follow, and I'd made it through casting."

Wyatt smiled at her. "Because you're so perfect?" he teased her.

"I think it was more that for some reason he saw me as the raw material he could work with to accomplish his vision."

"You were his clay?"

"That seemed to be what he thought I *could* be. Or at least what he was looking for. I can't say I was thrilled to be seen that way, but maybe it comes with the territory. I need to be pretty accepting of other people's needs and weaknesses, to accommodate them to some degree. Maybe he thought he could put that to work for him."

"What did this Svengali want from you?"

"Svengali?" Neily repeated, laughing slightly, wryly, at that notion of Trent. "There was no hypnotism or evil intent that I was aware of, but, yes, he was definitely manipulative. He got across what he wanted subtly and insidiously—at first, anyway. He'd make suggestions that just seemed pretty simple. Like, had I ever considered cutting my hair to make it less time-consuming to get ready in the morning. Or would I consider folding the towels like he did because they fit better in the linen closet."

"So it wasn't criticism so much as him being helpful?"

"Mmm," Neily said, knowing she was beginning to sound slightly forlorn as she mentally relived a very negative part of her past. "And I was willing to give some things a shot or concede to things that didn't seem like a big deal to me—I didn't care how the towels were folded, so, since it mattered to him, I did it his way."

"But it didn't stop there," Wyatt guessed, sounding genuinely sympathetic now.

"No. And the longer it went on the worse it got. The

more controlling and dictatorial *he* got. He decided I should stop working for Social Services and go into private practice with him, that we should be the married counselors who did marriage counseling."

"You didn't want to do that?"

"I like the variety of things I do—I like counseling, including marriage counseling—but I like the other parts of my job as a social worker, too. And I started to see that what Trent had in mind was me sitting primly beside him on a couch as the example of the good wife that other women should aspire to be. A mannequin might have accomplished the same thing."

Okay, maybe that was a little bitter. Neily tempered it.

"And as things went on it got worse. And more personal. I'd come out dressed for a party, for instance, and he'd take one look and do an assessment. He'd criticize my clothes, my makeup—everything. Then, on the way to the party, he'd give instructions like *make sure you remember not to ask so many questions, not to laugh too loudly, to let me do the talking*—"

"You were supposed to dress and do your makeup according to his specifications, and then go somewhere and be seen and not heard?" Wyatt asked in amazement.

"Basically."

"He wanted you to be *the little woman*—like something out of the fifties?"

Neily shrugged again, feeling more melancholy than she'd thought this could still make her feel. "That was his vision of the perfect wife. Anyway, I finally realized that he was trying to mold me to fit that image, that it wasn't me he wanted at all, that I was just... Well, what I said before, the raw material he could work with to shape his ideal mate. And that was when I got out."

"I don't know," Wyatt mused. "I'm thinking *crazy* might be a good description of this guy."

"Neurotic, anyway," Neily conceded. "And then I had to worry a little afterward about myself and why I'd gotten involved in a relationship that wasn't altogether healthy."

"It doesn't sound like it was unhealthy on your part," Wyatt concluded. "Adapting and compromising has to happen on both sides of any match. But I haven't seen anything about you that should be changed, let alone to fit someone's fantasy. He should have been glad for what he had."

Okay, that chased away most of the melancholies and made her smile.

"*Glad* for what he *had*... You're so poetic," she teased, in order to lighten the tone.

Wyatt returned her smile and played along. "Your nose is like a rose. Your eyes are like pies. Your—"

"Okay, enough!" Neily said, laughing at his silliness.

He sobered somewhat again and cast her another sympathetic look. "I'm sorry if you were hurt. But the guy really couldn't have been too smart if he didn't appreciate you."

"Well, that's true!" she agreed with mock enthusiasm to keep things light.

A loud clap of thunder startled Neily just then and caused them both to look to the sky. There had been predictions for torrential rains tonight. As the first drops began to fall, they returned to Boone's ranch house.

When they got there guests were beginning to leave amidst jokes about the potential for rain so hard the road would wash out, stranding everyone there with the bride and groom for their wedding night.

It *was* late and it had been a long day for Neily, so she was ready to go, too. Since she'd driven out with her brother Jon rather than taking her own car, Wyatt persuaded her to let him drive her home.

They ended up giving Neily's next-door neighbor a ride, too, leaving conversation on the drive all about the wedding. It allowed Neily time to consider whether or not to invite Wyatt in when they reached her house.

She wanted to. There was no doubt about that.

But talking about Trent had reminded her that she needed to keep things with Wyatt purely friendly. There was the whole resemblance to his late wife. The fact that there *was* a late wife. And while the ghost of a late wife might not be the same as what had happened with Trent, she was afraid to take the risk that the situations might be anything at all similar.

By the time they pulled into her drive she thought she had a handle on the urge to ask him in. The weather predictions had proved right—rain was coming down hard. Neily's neighbor had brought an umbrella and assured them she would be fine as she crossed the front yards to get home. But Wyatt insisted on using his suit coat to shield Neily in a mad dash to her front porch.

Still, she wasn't going to ask him in, she swore to herself. And she tried to make that clear to him by unlocking and opening her front door but staying out on the porch to turn and say what she intended to be a quick and simple thanks and good-night.

But before she could do that, Wyatt said, "Tell me what I'm in for tomorrow with this other social worker."

It wasn't quite as cold in the shelter of the porch as it had been in the open of her brother's barnyard. So when Wyatt moved to put his coat around her shoulders again she declined the offer, insisting that he take it back.

As he put it on she tried not to feast on the sight of muscular shoulders stretching the seams of his shirt when he put his arms in the sleeves, or the way his chest swelled against the smooth front.

She tried, but she wasn't too successful and only belatedly remembered that he'd asked her a question about Saturday when her supervisor would make the home visit Neily had told him was coming.

"It'll be the same as talking to me or talking to the social worker you met with before you left Missoula," she explained once she'd forced her eyes off his body. "Cheryl is the coordinator and supervisor on your case, so she wants to meet with you and Theresa and Mary Pat personally. She'll talk to each of you separately, and she'll ask you the same questions you've answered over and over again. There shouldn't be any surprises."

"Will you be there?"

Neily shook her head, trying hard to stick strictly to business and not think about how the yellow glow of light flooding through her open front door made him look like some kind of gold-plated statue of masculine beauty.

"I'm scheduled to meet with Cheryl afterward," she said simply.

"What about later? Will you come by to visit Gram?"

Was he just trying to find out what was on the next day's agenda or was he asking when he would be seeing her again?

It gave her a little thrill to think he might be trying to figure out when he was going to see her. But the very fact that it thrilled her was all the more reason *not* to see him. "Actually, I'm not working this weekend. Cheryl will see you guys tomorrow, and Sunday I'm driving down to Wyoming to have lunch with my own grandmother."

"I remember now," he said. Then his eyebrows arched as if she'd said something surprising. "Are you saying I won't see you the whole weekend?"

She tamped down on the rush she got from the hint of disappointment in his voice.

"You get the weekend off," she said.

"Huh..." he mused. "What if I don't want the weekend off?"

"Because you love to be under the watchful eye of Social Services? Now *that's* unhealthy," she joked. "But you'll still get some of that tomorrow, with Cheryl."

"Not the same," he complained.

"Careful," she pretended to warn. "You don't want me thinking that you can't be on your own."

"It isn't the being on my own that's the problem." He reached both hands to her shoulders, rubbing slowly, sensually up and down her arms. "Come on, you'll miss me, too, and you know it," he teased with a tilted, devilish smile.

"In just two days?"

"Two long, long, lonely days..." he said with so much mock misery she laughed again.

"Are you worried that you won't survive?" she goaded.

"There's a real possibility. Here I am, alone in a strange place, knowing almost no one, without even a clue where to turn in case of a crisis, a troubled grandmother on my hands, abandoned by the one person—"

"Oh, that is a sad story," she said of what sounded like a bad movie teaser. "Have I told you that part of my job is weeding out the drama when someone is just playing me?"

He grinned. "But isn't my desperate attempt for pity reason enough for the social worker to pay a visit?"

"Shameless," she decreed. Just before she caved. "Maybe I'll stop by in the afternoon tomorrow," she said as if she were doing him a favor.

He grinned even bigger. "Better."

It felt better to her, too. Heaven help her...

His hands had slowed their massage of her arms, settling in one place to let his thumbs alone brush feathery strokes along her bare skin.

His eyes glinted as they held hers, and despite warning herself to say good-night and go inside, she stayed right where she was, just wanting him to kiss her again.

"Cheryl could be there really early in the morning," she said in a feeble attempt to cut this short. "So you should go home and get some rest. You don't want to be all bleary-eyed when you meet her."

"No, I wouldn't want that," he agreed as if he were so distracted by the study of her face that what she said was only registering peripherally.

"Thanks for the ride," she tried.

"Thanks for tonight," he countered.

"It was my brother's wedding. I was just there," she said. But it wouldn't have been the same for her if *he* hadn't been.

Oh, yeah, I'm in trouble.

He pulled her toward him then, leaning in to kiss her. He wrapped his arms around her, making a cocoon of that big, warm male body she had been enthralled with only moments earlier.

Her arms went around him, too, slipping between the silky lining of his jacket and the crisp fabric of his dress shirt, and she pressed her palms to his broad back.

His lips parted more and his tongue came to deepen the kiss, taking them to a new level. Circling and tempting and enticing—there was nothing chaste about that kiss. Or that tongue, plundering, pillaging, ravaging her mouth with his until her head was lighter even than the champagne had left it, until that kiss wreaked havoc with every thought, stripping her bare of any notion of ever ending it.

Until Wyatt slowly pulled away, leaving her slightly breathless and weak and wanting more as he raised his head just enough to peer down into her eyes again.

"I have to see you tomorrow," he said as if to make that clear in case she doubted it.

Neily nodded because she couldn't summon her voice and at that moment all she could think about was having him kiss her like that again.

But he didn't.

Instead his hands went back to her arms and he straightened up, putting some distance between them, enough for Neily to draw her hands to the sides of his waist.

"Go in before I can't let you," he commanded.

Neily raised her chin in concession, found just enough voice to whisper, "Good night," and stepped back.

Where she watched Wyatt walk out to his SUV in no hurry despite the rain.

She had the feeling that he was using it as nature's cold shower and wondered if she should take a walk out there, too.

Except she knew if she did she might not be able to keep herself from dragging him back to the house with her.

She managed to keep herself rooted to her front porch while he got into his car, restarted the engine and finally drove away, leaving her heart pounding hard and fast...

And her eagerly awaiting tomorrow.

Chapter Ten

Saturday did not end up being a day off for Neily. She spent the morning writing her formal report on the Graysons and had lunch with her supervisor. Then she went to check on Miss Sela. While she was there she organized the many casseroles, pies and bundt cakes that had been sent by friends and neighbors, staying long enough to heat one of the meals and keep Miss Sela company through the elderly woman's dinner.

It was after dark by the time she left and she still hadn't made good on her word to Wyatt to stop by.

Should she or shouldn't she—that was the argument she had with herself from the minute she got in her car in front of Miss Sela's house until she parked in the driveway at Theresa's.

Probably she shouldn't but she was anyway—that was the conclusion.

All for nothing.

Wyatt wasn't there and Theresa was already asleep for the night, Mary Pat told her.

So Neily was on her way home. Wondering where Wyatt was and feeling much more disappointed and dejected than she should have been.

And then she drove up to her own house and there he was. His SUV was parked in her driveway and he was sitting on her front porch with a grocery sack between his feet.

"I just came from your place," she said in greeting when she got out of the car and headed for the house.

"I gave up on you," he answered.

"I've been with Miss Sela all afternoon."

Neily stopped at the base of the stairs, unable to control how happy she was to see him.

He had on faded blue jeans and a brown V-neck sweater over a white crewneck T-shirt—nothing special, and yet to her he was a sight for sore eyes.

"I'm sure you know we've gotten the stamp of approval from Social Services—since you were part of giving it," he said.

"Plus I had lunch with Cheryl and she told me," Neily said as if she hadn't known the day before that it was coming. "Congratulations."

"I wanted to thank you—"

"There's no need. I didn't see any reason for alarm

and that's what I reported. Neither did the caseworker in Missoula, so it wasn't only me."

"It was you here," he insisted. "And you who stayed with Gram before I could get here, you who's done a lot more than that since then. If we were in Missoula, I would have called you and told you to put on something flashy, and then I would have taken you to the perfect restaurant. But here my hands were tied, so I had to cater it." He peered down into the sack.

Neily craned forward for a look, too. "I can't tell what's in there."

"I talked to your brother Cam to find out what your favorite foods are and got them together. From the looks of it, I might have been on the wrong track if I'd gone the Missoula route."

"Corn dogs with five-alarm chili to dip them in, sour pickles, potato salad—"

"And an ice cream cake—chocolate mint cake with a layer of mint chocolate-chip ice cream."

Neily couldn't keep from grinning. "It's what I have every birthday."

"Well, it isn't fancy, but it's all in here. So what do you say? Can I thank you over dinner?"

"I *am* hungry, and even if it isn't my birthday there's nothing I like better than a good corn dog."

Wyatt laughed, picked up the bag and stood. "I'm told Adz makes the best one in town and I got all the food there," he said, then turned to the side and ushered her ahead of him with a wave of his free arm.

Neily took the lead, unlocking her front door and

letting them both in. She flipped on the lights and closed the door behind him.

"Tell me where to go, give me a minute to set up and then make a grand entrance and pretend to be surprised," he instructed.

"The kitchen is in back," she explained. "The dining room is next to it—you choose where you want to eat."

"Oh, for this we *have* to eat in the dining room," he deadpanned. "But it might take five or ten minutes for me to get it all ready."

"Great, I'll freshen up," she said.

From her spot in the entryway, she watched as he went down the hall beside the staircase, telling him where to find the light switch once he reached the kitchen.

"Think you can take it from there?" she called.

"I'll be fine. Just make yourself scarce."

Still unable to suppress a smile, Neily nearly ran up the stairs to her room.

She'd already dressed today with the idea that she might see him, so she didn't bother changing out of the lemonade-colored square-necked T-shirt she was wearing over a pair of khaki twill pants that hugged every curve. But she did run a brush through her hair to leave it falling free, and refreshed her blush and mascara. Then she applied a light lipstick and sprayed her most expensive perfume into the air so she could walk through it.

All the while asking herself what she thought she was doing...

But in truth she knew what she was doing. She was

getting ready to spend the evening with a man she just couldn't seem to refuse no matter how hard she tried. And now that there was no longer any conflict of interest?

She was putting on perfume instead of telling him they didn't need to see each other anymore.

"Just give up," she beseeched her reflection in the mirror above the dresser in her bedroom.

She wanted to do this. No matter how ill-advised, or how stupid. She wanted a little time with this guy.

Just a little...

Was that so much to ask?

She hadn't met anyone she'd felt this way about in a long time, and she wasn't getting anywhere trying to fight it, so why keep beating herself up over it?

Besides, if Wyatt was the first guy she'd been attracted to since Trent, didn't that make Wyatt a mere transition for her? A bridge to help her cross back into the swing of things?

She knew she needed to get out there again, and until now no one had even tempted her to, so didn't she need to run with that?

Okay, maybe she was rationalizing. But there was some merit to it just the same.

And, really, wasn't that what was going on for Wyatt, too? She didn't know for sure, because she hadn't sifted through his past the way he'd sifted through hers, but she had the impression that he hadn't dated anyone since his wife's death. If that was true, then that made her *his* transitional person. And if she went in knowing that, keeping her eyes wide open, maybe this could work to both their advantages, ease them both back into the race and make their time together of mutual benefit.

Theoretically she thought it was possible. And at that moment, when she couldn't wait to get back downstairs and be with him again, she didn't see anything wrong with them sharing a path that would take them both out of the remnants of painful pasts and launch them on their way to better futures.

Some time. Some food. Some talk. Some kissing. Big deal.

As long as she was well aware that it didn't have a lengthy shelf life, why couldn't she indulge herself now that the issue of working with him wasn't a problem?

She thought she could. And she was going to.

Just a little socializing with a gorgeous man who had happened into her life for the moment. Definitely not a big deal unless she let it become one. And she wouldn't. Simple as that.

"And there's nothing wrong with it," she said as she took a deep breath that puffed out her chest.

With her mind made up, she smoothed her low-cut T-shirt, and, before she could chicken out, spun away from the mirror and went to see what Wyatt had waiting for her.

"Voila! Corn dogs by candlelight," Wyatt announced when Neily found him in her dining room.

Three tall tapers provided the only light. They were situated at one end of the long oval antique table, between two place settings of her family's best china and an array of take-out food.

Neily went to the chair he was holding for her. "I see you found the good tablecloth and china and silver."

"All in that cupboard over there."

"The sideboard," Neily corrected as he sat just around the curve of the table so they were partially facing each other.

She'd been wearing a jacket when she'd arrived home, so this was the first he'd seen of her T-shirt. Neily saw his eyes drop to her neckline for just a split second. She felt herself flush slightly, but she didn't think he could tell that she was blushing in the candle-light and she was grateful for that.

"My mother would have a fit if she knew we were using this stuff for anything but a holiday or a major celebration," she said, referring to the good china again.

"I won't tell if you don't," Wyatt said. Using silver tongs, he served her a corn dog and a pickle, then picked up a matching ladle for the chili and another matching serving spoon for the potato salad.

"Do you live here alone?" he asked once they both had a helping of everything but the cake and had begun to eat.

"For now," Neily answered after her initial taste of chili-dipped corn dog. "The seven of us—me, Boone, Cam, Taylor, Jon, Scott and Mara—all inherited the house equally, so we all own it, and we all sort of move in and out as our lives go in one direction or another—"

"An open-door policy?"

"Right."

"So who's in charge of maintenance or decorating or upkeep?"

Neily was glad to see that he was unflinchingly eating the hottest chili Northbridge had to offer. "Whoever lives here or is available pitches in if the place needs paint or repair, if the lawn needs mowing or tree branches have to be cut. As for the decorating, a lot of the furniture was my mother's, but things that get wear and tear have so far been replaced by Mara or me—my brothers couldn't care less if there's a hole in the couch."

"It's a nice place," Wyatt said, glancing around. "Homey. Warm. Comfortable."

"Are those polite ways of saying it's old and lived in?" she joked.

"No, I really like it."

"What do you have in Missoula—a house, an apartment?" she asked then, deciding it was time to get some of her own curiosity appeased.

"I have a house I bought when Mikayla and I got married. Mikayla was…unique. She had strong ideas about decorating and an apartment just wouldn't do."

Neily certainly hadn't had any inclination that Mikayla was at all unusual. She considered herself ordinary and if she brought the other woman to mind for Theresa and Wyatt, how could the other woman be unique…?

"How so?" she asked.

Wyatt smiled as if the memory amused him. "I met Mikayla when we were building a Home-Max in San Francisco."

"Did she work for you?"

"She would have considered it creatively stifling to work in a place like Home-Max. We actually met in a grocery store during an earthquake. I yanked her out of the way of a rack of soup cans that was about to fall on her."

Neily chuckled a little, keeping with the lighter vein in which he was talking about his past. "That's not something you hear every day."

"But it seemed so fitting for Mikayla."

"Because she was unique," Neily reminded, trying to keep her tone matter-of-fact when she said it.

"She was a little out there in some ways," Wyatt added, again with a nostalgic smile. "She dressed—day and night—like she was going to a cocktail party. She said everything should make a statement, so she always wore four-inch heels to give her stature. She had six holes pierced in her right ear and only one in her left to let people know she had a busy, bustling, active side but also a serene, go-with-the-flow, nature-loving side, too."

"Yin and yang?"

"She had a tattoo of that on the back of her neck. But beyond the show that was Mikayla, she was also sweet and giving. She had amazing patience with Gram because she was very accepting of everyone, of any flaw or quirk. She was…" He laughed slightly. "She was Mikayla. She was great."

And a lot for anyone who followed her to live up to…

Neily had a sudden understanding of why she hadn't been thrilled about hearing her praises of Trent the night before, because she couldn't say she was thrilled to hear such glowing things about his late wife.

To get him past that, she said, "So you saved her from being clobbered by soup cans. Then what?"

"She thanked me by buying me coffee when the quake was over and—" He sighed and shrugged. "That was it—there was an instant chemistry between us."

"You rushed out and got married four hours later?" Neily asked, joking.

"Not quite. But we saw each other every day from then on. We were married before the store was finished—two months later."

Talking about his wife was slowing down his appetite for his second corn dog, but now that Neily had him started on this road, she felt strongly that there were things she should know.

"And when the store was finished you moved her from San Francisco to Missoula where she had different decorating tastes than your family?" she said to remind him where in the conversation he'd detoured.

"Pretty much," he said, but he didn't seem to balk at answering her questions, and Neily appreciated that he was being open with her.

"Like I said, Mikayla was unique. She was an artist and in San Francisco she worked in a gallery that specialized in abstract anything. Most of that kind of art is a mystery to me—a bunch of auto parts glued together just looks like auto parts glued together, if you ask me. But the weirder the piece, the better she liked it. By the time we got back to Missoula she was doing fewer paintings and sculptures herself, but she wanted to start a gallery to show other people's work. Her own creative outlet became our house and her taste for the contemporary stuff came out there—sometimes when she bought something it was tough to tell whether it was a piece of artwork or something I was supposed to sit on. Everything had to be cutting-edge…"

Why did that seem to make sadness creep over him?

"You didn't like it?" Neily guessed as she pushed her plate away. As much as she'd enjoyed the food, she'd had enough and was far more interested in what Wyatt was telling her.

He shrugged again. "I didn't care. I mean, plumbing fixtures and hardware I know, but artwork and ottomans? I think in terms of comfort, not style. As long as I had my big leather recliner in front of the entertainment center in the den, she could do what she wanted. And she did."

"You say you were okay with that but you still make it sound like a bad thing," Neily observed.

Wyatt pushed away his plate, too. "We'd been married about two years when Mikayla got pregnant. One of the artwork-slash-furniture pieces she'd brought home was a coffee table. It was this strange cubic conglomeration. Anyway, it was full of sharp edges and we knew it was going to have to go when the baby came because it wouldn't be safe to have a kid around something like that. It never occurred to us that it posed a danger otherwise…"

Wyatt paused for a drink of iced tea, obviously not finding it easy to tell the story now.

Neily couldn't imagine where he was going with it and so she just waited, giving him the time he needed.

After the drink he sighed and continued.

"Then, one day when Mikayla was eight months pregnant I went to work as usual, leaving her home alone, getting dressed to go to her gallery…as usual. About eleven that morning I got a call from the woman who worked at the gallery with her, wanting to know where Mikayla was, if she hadn't come in because she was having the baby early and I'd forgotten to let her know…"

Another pause and Neily thought she could almost feel the fear that must have run through him at the time. Certainly his face was tight, his entire body seemed tense, and rather than looking at her, he was staring daggers at the glass of iced tea that his left hand had in a stranglehold.

"I called Mary Pat right away," he went on with an echo of the panic that he must have experienced then. "She rushed over while I drove like a maniac to get home. By the time I got there an ambulance had already arrived but there was nothing anybody could do. From the looks of it, Mikayla had tripped—probably because she had on those damn high heels that she wasn't supposed to wear that late in her pregnancy, and because she was always barreling around the place, in a hurry…"

He shook his head so sadly it made Neily's heart break. Then in a deep, quiet voice, he said, "She'd fallen on that damn coffee table—belly first. The paramedics said she had the kind of injury they see in pregnant women in car accidents—the fall and the way she'd hit had ruptured her uterus. There were signs that she'd tried to get to a phone, but she must have been in too much pain. She and the baby had bled to death."

"I'm so sorry!" Neily nearly whispered.

"It was bad," Wyatt admitted. "In the blink of an eye a time in my life that I thought was perfect and happy and only getting happier and more perfect…it just crashed." He was still staring at the glass but his brows arched and he shook his head in what appeared to be disbelief. "I wasn't too sure I was going to make it."

"How long ago was this?" Neily asked gently.

"Two years. Sometimes it seems like a lifetime. Sometimes it seems like yesterday."

"I can imagine," Neily commiserated. "Just like that, to lose your wife and your baby…"

"Yeah, I lost everything, including myself and my sanity for a while," he said. "I'm not sure how I got through the funeral—I don't think I would have without Ry and Marti. Then there are weeks right after that that I don't even remember. I bottomed out worse than I thought was possible. I took a sledge-hammer to nearly every piece of furniture in the house. Drank too much. Put my fist through a door. Thought about…"

He cut himself off and sat up straighter, as if he were dragging himself out of those desperate days all over again. Then he pivoted in his chair and braced an arm across the back of it.

"I'll tell you what," he said then. "I gained a whole

new sympathy for my grandmother. And a whole new worry for what might be genetic."

"Her depression?" Neily asked.

Wyatt nodded solemnly. "I spent some time there and it isn't fun."

"You spent time grieving and going through a depression that's only to be expected after a loss like you experienced. Theresa's condition is an illness."

"One I don't want," he said more to himself than to her for no reason Neily understood.

"No one would want to suffer the way Theresa does," Neily agreed. "But while you got an unfortunate taste of some of it, it isn't like inheriting her eye color. A big indicator that your depression is different from your grandmother's is that you came out of yours."

"But what if I hadn't?" he said.

"*What if* isn't the point. The point is that you did. That you were able to. Your reaction was normal, and you fought your way out of grief just like you were supposed to," she assured him, because it was clear it weighed on him.

He smiled very slightly, as if he appreciated what she was saying. But she still wasn't sure he was buying it.

"I'm serious," she insisted.

His smile grew. "Well, you are more of an expert than I am. Will you put it in writing? Give me a clean bill of mental health?"

Now he was joking again and Neily saw that as a good sign.

"Absolutely. I'll even get it notarized," she promised.

Glad that things had lightened up again, Neily was less glad when she heard her front door open and her brother Cam's voice call her name.

"I'm sorry, I completely forgot—I asked Cam to come by tonight and switch cars with me so I can drive his SUV to Wyoming tomorrow since there's a chance of snow."

"Hey, if it gets us off *this* topic he can even have a corn dog," Wyatt said. Then, with a nod in the direction of the dining-room entrance, he added, "Do what you need to do. I wouldn't let you lift a finger for cleanup anyway since this fancy feast was in your honor."

"I'll only be a minute," she assured him.

"Go ahead," Wyatt urged, standing and beginning to collect the plates.

"I'll be right back."

"I'll be at the kitchen sink, washing dishes and trying not to break your mother's good china," he said. "And from here on tonight, no gloom!"

That was an order Neily was only too willing to accept as she went to answer her brother's call—and wondered what else Wyatt had in store for their evening.

Chapter Eleven

There shouldn't have been anything sexy about a man standing at her counter making a bad attempt to cut a cake. And yet when Neily returned to the kitchen after having traded car keys with Cam, sexy was just how Wyatt looked to her.

Tall, straight of back, broad of shoulder, narrow of waist and with a derriere to die for. And more than ice cream cake, what she wanted was to see him without his clothes on....

Neily yanked herself out of that thought and joined him at the counter where he was mutilating her cake.

"There's an easier way to do that," she informed him.

"Chainsaw?" he said as if that was what he was considering next.

"That would probably work, too, but a knife heated in hot water is a little less bulky."

She demonstrated the technique and produced two neat slices of the chocolate mint cake.

"You're full of surprises," Wyatt marveled with barely a glance over his shoulder at what she'd done.

He'd turned his back to the counter beside her and was leaning there with his arms crossed over his chest. It was really Neily he was looking at and his expression was relaxed again. There wasn't so much as a hint of the shadows of sadness, grief or remorse that had been there when they'd been talking about the death of his wife and unborn baby.

"Not to bring up that topic you wanted off of when Cam came," she said, referring to Wyatt's comment when her brother had interrupted them earlier. "But are you okay?"

"You mean, because we talked about Mikayla and the baby?"

Neily nodded as she put the cake on two everyday dishes.

"It's not my favorite subject, but I can talk about it without any long-lasting effects."

"Good," Neily said, handing him one of the dessert plates. "Let's eat it in the living room where we can be more comfortable."

She took the lead, sitting sideways on the sofa when she got there, her legs tucked under her.

Wyatt sat facing her, one of his thick thighs on the cushion between them, his ankle braced on his other knee.

"Can I ask two more questions?" she said as they ate their cake. Since she'd gone this far into the subject of his late wife, she thought she might as well have the rest of her curiosity appeased.

"About Mikayla?"

"Sort of."

"Sure," he conceded.

"One—have you dated or been involved with anybody since?"

Wyatt shook his head. "Neither."

She'd thought as much. All the more reason to believe this…flirtation really was just a transition for them both.

"Two," she said then. "After hearing you describe Mikayla, I can't see where she and I are at all alike."

"Nobody said you were alike." Wyatt frowned at her as if she were out of her mind.

"Theresa confuses me with her all the time," Neily said defensively.

"You can't go by Gram. Half the time she thinks I'm Ry or that Ry is me."

"But *you've* said there was a resemblance, too," Neily insisted.

"It's not as if you're Mikayla's doppelganger. That'd be creepy. You have the same hair color and there's some similarity in the cheekbones and around the nose," he said, motioning to those parts of her face with his free hand. "But now that I've met your sister—and even your half sister—the same could be said about them. There are just a few surface catch-it-out-of-the-corner-of-the-eye kinds of things. And to tell you the truth, I'm seeing it less and less. Now when I see you, I only see…you."

He finished his cake and leaned over to set the dish on the coffee table. When he straightened up again he stretched an arm along the top of the rear sofa cushions.

"I guess there are a few other similarities, though," he said then. "You're as nice as Mikayla was. As patient with Gram and as accepting of her—not everyone is. Marti, Ry and I have all brought people around to meet her who have been uncomfortable. But you're more…down-to-earth."

"I'm definitely not artsy," Neily agreed as she set her own plate beside his on the coffee table and settled back on her haunches.

"You're calmer, too. More quiet."

"More boring?"

He smiled. "I haven't been bored so far. If I had, you might be able to keep me away. But here I am…"

In all his glory, Neily thought as she drank in the sight of those finely chiseled features, that couldn't-care-less-but-perfect-anyway hair, those eyes that were such a sultry gray, that body that made everything inside of her stand up and take notice…

Wyatt's voice interrupted her train of thought. "How about giving me a tour of this place? I've never been in a house with a turret."

"Okay," Neily agreed, deciding she was also ready to leave behind the subject of his past.

"So besides the turret, is there a dungeon, too?" he asked as they both stood.

Neily laughed again. "There's a basement no one wants to see, but no dungeon, no. And you've already been in the living room, the dining room, and the kitchen—that's about all there is on this floor except what's inside the turret at this level."

She led him across the Victorian-style entryway and opened the door at the base of the stairs. "It *might* have been a torture chamber once upon a time," she said very ominously, as if she were the guide in a haunted house. "But now we use it as a combination..." she paused for dramatic effect "...den, office and TV room."

"Ooo, spooky," Wyatt said as they went in.

Then, in a normal tone, he added, "I'm guessing your family didn't build the place if you don't know where the torture chamber could have been."

"The house is one of Northbridge's originals," Neily answered. "My mother's parents died when she was young and left her a little money. She came here and used the inheritance to buy this and a dry-cleaning business that we still own."

"Your father wasn't in on the buying of the house and business?" Wyatt inquired. They left the den and climbed the wide staircase that rose and then curved to the second level.

"No, thank goodness. If my mother had had to sell the house to split things up I don't know what would have happened. She met my father after she'd moved here and invested her money. Like the house, my father was already a fixture—he was a Northbridge native."

"And your mom ended up staying, but your dad didn't?"

"Right. Whether it was wanderlust or small-town claustrophobia or just that seven kids were too many for him, he took off and left her to raise us alone."

"Did he visit after that? Did you go to stay with him?"

"Nope. He left and that was it—no child support, no contact."

"But you kept in touch with your grandmother on that side—you did say it was your father's mother you're going to see tomorrow, right?"

"Right. And, yes, my grandmother on that side did keep in touch. As best she could. Both of my grandparents were mortified when my father left us. And in a small town it's hard to hold your head up when you know everyone, they know you and you're the talk of the town. I was too young to remember, but in the middle of all the stress and upset my grandfather had a stroke. He was left bedridden and needed to be in a nursing home. Northbridge doesn't have that kind of facility but there was one in Sheridan, so that's where he had to be placed. My grandmother moved there to be near him and look after him, but she visited us, we visited her, and there's always been contact."

"But not much help for your mom from that quarter."

"No. My grandmother had her hands full with my grandfather until he died six years ago. But we did okay," Neily finished on a more positive note.

They'd reached the top of the stairs just before that

and he was giving her an appreciative smile that went through Neily like warm honey. It took some willpower for her to break the glance that held hers and continue the tour.

"Those are bedrooms there, there, there and there," she said, pointing them out from where they were standing in the open area at the center of five doorways. Then she went to the fifth door and led him through that one. "And in the turret up here is the playroom… Well, actually as teenagers we called it the recreation room because *playroom* sounded too babyish, but mostly we still fall back into calling it the playroom."

She flipped the light switch and on went the Tiffany lamp that hung above the pool table, giving a multihued but dim glow to the very large space.

Wyatt seemed more interested in that use of the turret space than he had been of the den's, and while he began to look around, Neily perched on the pool table, her legs dangling over the side.

"You must have every board game in existence," he said when he looked over the shelves of boxes against one wall.

"With seven kids my mom was desperate to keep us occupied."

"Darts, pinball, foosball," he said as he moved on, going from one to the other.

"And there's a top that can be put over the pool table here for Ping-Pong—Boone and Taylor are maniacs for playing each other." Neily pointed to a chalkboard with her brothers' names on it and several rows of slash marks below them. "They keep a running score and none of us *dares* to mess with it."

"This must be the newer-additions section—video games," Wyatt observed as he sauntered over to that portion of the playroom.

Neily wiggled her thumbs at him as if she were working a controller. "I'm the champion if you want to try to take me on," she bragged.

Not until Wyatt grinned a lascivious grin did she realize how that had sounded.

"Maybe later," he said in a voice that raised her temperature another notch, even though she knew he was just playing along.

He'd hit all the high points of the room then and he came to join her at the pool table, leaning against it and stretching his long legs out to cross at the ankles, bracing himself at a slant.

Neily turned to face him, one of her legs curved between them so he wasn't just looking at her profile.

"Yep," he said then. "I like your little town and your big old house. And I kind of like you, too," he continued, as if it wasn't easy for him to come to grips with that fact.

"Kind of? Oh, be still my heart," she said facetiously.

He grinned broadly, lines crinkling at the corners of eyes that peered up at her with a mischievous glimmer.

"It's funny, isn't it?" he said then. "For years my grandmother wouldn't even go outside to collect her own mail, but she got herself all the way to Northbridge and here we are, you and I. We probably wouldn't have ever known the other existed otherwise. It makes you wonder…" It didn't make her wonder as much as it filled her with a whole new kind of warmth. And that was when she reminded herself that she'd given herself permission to stop resisting him.

She bent over slowly and kissed him, the kind of kiss they'd shared the first time—chaste, sweet, light—unsure where she was going with it.

But Wyatt didn't wait to find out. As his free hand came to cup the back of her head he took control from there.

His lips parted and his tongue teased hers into parting, too, so he could slip inside to toy, to taunt, to entice her into sensual play.

Not that it took much persuasion, because Neily was willing to give as good as she got.

Mouths opened wider and grew hungrier and more insistent, and Wyatt's big hand held her to it all while his fingers wove through her hair.

Neily placed a palm to the hard wall of his chest as she became increasingly aware of her own breasts aching in response. Of the growing yearning to feel his hands on her body…

Her mouth opened wider and their kiss went from sensual to plain, outright sexy. Wyatt's hand slid from her hair to the side of her neck, then to her collarbone. Tentative, careful—she knew he was giving her the chance to move that hand before he went any farther. But she didn't. Instead she took a deep breath that pushed her into his grasp.

It was all the encouragement he needed, and that hand dropped an inch more to take her fully within his grip, to bring one tightened nipple to the center of his palm.

She let her own hand glide underneath his sweater, pulling his T-shirt free of the waistband, and finally felt the sleek smoothness of his flesh, of his satiny skin over the honed muscles of his back.

As if that had given him license, his hand abandoned her breast only long enough to slip underneath her T-shirt, too, to find her again without that between them.

But her bra still stood in the way. At least it did until he scooped her breast out of the cup.

Nothing had ever felt so good. Strong and gentle. Just rough enough. Just light enough. Just right. He had a wondrous touch and he knew how to use it, where to use it, when to tease, when to torment, when to give exactly what she needed.

He rose up enough to put himself on the pool table with her, then wrapped his other arm around her and eased her down so he could lean over her. He went on kissing her, too, although now it was more a raw plundering of her mouth with his and his with hers.

She had his sweater and T-shirt up high enough to expose his side, his flat belly, his chest, and while she wanted his shirt and sweater gone completely, she didn't want to break away for even the moment it would take to get them off. So she left them as she ravaged his back, his pecs, his ribs, reveling in the contours of that body she had yet to see.

Maybe she should take the time, she thought, and break away long enough to tear his shirts off, to shed her own, to get rid of the rest of his clothes and hers…

She was alive with wanting him. Her entire being was screaming for his touch. For his kiss. For his mouth and tongue and teeth. And she was desperate to see him, to do everything to him that she wanted done to her, to get to know every part of his body with her own.

More. She was starving for more. For all of it. For clothes to be thrown to the floor. For him to take her breasts into his mouth. For the feel of him in her hand. Inside of her…

So what if they were in the playroom, on the pool table? So what if she didn't have protection and he probably didn't, either. So what, if only she could have him!

Now! Right this minute!

But even in the midst of that demand from within her, a tiny voice of reason made itself known.

She might have conceded to her attraction to Wyatt being a transition for her, but that didn't mean that a heartbeat later she should go ahead and rip off his clothes and let him make love to her on the pool table.

Did it?

No, she knew it didn't.

Unfortunately…

It took every ounce of will she had, but she stopped. She stopped digging her fingers into his back. Stopped kissing him with such abandon and finessed them out of what had only been escalating before.

Wyatt got the message. After a last, lingering caress of her breast, he brought his hand out from under her shirt. Then his mouth deserted hers completely.

"So, no, huh?" he asked in a gravelly voice, a wry half smile on his lips, and no need to clarify what he was talking about.

"Probably not the best idea, no."

"I don't know, seems like a pretty good one to me," he nearly groaned.

But then he rolled to lie flat on his back on the pool table. She rolled to her back, too, and fought her own intense urge to just say the heck with it and climb on top of him.

They lay there in silence for a while before Wyatt jumped off the pool table.

"Sometimes I think there are forces at work here that are bigger than we are," he said.

"I understand *that* feeling," she concurred. It certainly explained what had just happened.

"I should go," he said, pivoting to stand between Neily's knees where they folded over the table's edge, taking her hands to pull her up, too.

When she got there she realized she was basically straddling him and once again she had to battle her own inclinations in order not to wrap her legs around him, reel him in and start all over again.

Maybe he had similar thoughts because he stepped back and pulled her to slide down from the table, too. Then he let go of her and put some distance between them.

"I do have an early day tomorrow," Neily muttered

in response, wishing her own voice was a little stronger and less breathless.

They headed out of the playroom and down the stairs to the entryway. "Speaking of that," Wyatt said, "I was thinking when you were with Cam—why don't you let me drive you to Wyoming tomorrow?"

"Why?" Neily asked as they reached the front door.

"So you wouldn't have to go alone. So we could talk to your grandmother together about mine…" He shrugged and smiled a smile that somehow seemed to reflect what had just passed between them. "So I could buy you dinner in a real restaurant."

"Ooo, don't let anyone hear you say you don't think Adz isn't a real restaurant. Those could be fighting words," she warned jokingly, trying not to think about what they'd just done. Or to want to do more of it.

"We could take my SUV instead of Cam's, and I could give you some time alone with your grand-mother—I don't want to horn in on your lunch. But then maybe I could meet you for coffee later, and when your grandmother has had her fill of us, we could have a night on the town—just you and me."

"A night on the town in Sheridan, Wyoming? I'm not sure what that would involve. It isn't New York, you know."

"Still," he persisted. "I think we could find a nice place to eat, maybe a club to go to afterward…"

The feel of his hands on her skin was still fresh. Neily didn't have a doubt that a night alone on the town—even in Sheridan, Wyoming—was a dangerous thing to agree to.

"And we'd still drive back here? Just late?" she heard herself ask as if that were safety net enough.

"Whatever you want," he assured her. "I heard the weather report earlier—snow flurries but not much accumulation—so we should be able to get home."

"Cam *did* have use for his SUV tomorrow. I'm sure he wouldn't mind getting it back," she said. It was just an excuse to give in to him. What she was really thinking about was spending the long drive to Wyoming with Wyatt; about having a nice, romantic dinner with him in a quiet restaurant where no one would know them or interrupt them, where it really would be— Sheridan, Wyoming, or not—a genuine, wining-and-dining date…

"So what do you say?" Wyatt asked when she'd let her thoughts wander for too long.

"Okay," she said as if she were agreeing to something forbidden.

"What time shall I pick you up?"

She told him and felt a tiny shiver of anticipation run up her spine. She knew she should probably take it as a warning but decided to ignore it instead.

Wyatt took her in his arms and gave her a parting kiss that did little to forestall her desires, then he was out the door.

"I'll see you in the morning," he said as he left. "Get some sleep."

Neily nodded as if that wouldn't be a problem.

But as she watched him walk to his SUV she knew it was going to be.

She knew she was in for a long, restless night.

Chapter Twelve

"Theresa Hobbs is back in Northbridge and you're her grandson. I can hardly believe it," Ruby Pratt marveled as she, Neily and Wyatt were served their coffees Sunday afternoon.

Wyatt had kept his word—he'd left Neily to have lunch alone with her grandmother, then met up with them later. They were now in a coffee shop within the retirement complex where Ruby lived.

Outside, the spring snow that had just started falling early that morning had changed from the predicted flurries to a substantial storm. But inside all was cozy at a table near the window.

"I told Nana about your grandmother," Neily informed Wyatt after her own grandmother had brought up the subject.

"I'm so sorry she's troubled," Ruby added.

"We're all sorry about that," Wyatt assured her.

Neily was fairly certain that he'd already won Ruby over when he'd commented on her youthful appearance after Neily introduced them. A tall, stocky woman, Ruby paid considerable attention to the hair she dyed a honey hue, to the makeup she applied impeccably and to the clothes she made sure were always in fashion.

"Did you know Theresa well?" Neily asked. Although she'd told her grandmother about Theresa's extraordinary reappearance in Northbridge and some of her emotional issues, they hadn't gotten into more than that before Wyatt had joined them.

"Theresa and I were best friends," Ruby said.

That surprised Neily, although she knew it shouldn't have. Her relationship with her grandmother hadn't been so close that she had any knowledge of her grandmother's girlhood.

"Really?" Wyatt said to Ruby.

"Oh, yes. We were like sisters. Our mothers put us in the sandbox to play together before we could even walk. We were in the same grade all through school. And as teenagers… Well, you know how girls can be. We *had* to see each other and talk about *everything*. We were always sleeping at each other's houses and keeping secrets. We were inseparable. At least before she lost her family."

"Theresa was in Northbridge after that, though, wasn't she?" Neily said. "From what we've gathered, about eleven months."

Ruby nodded. "That sounds about right."

"Were you *not* inseparable after she lost her family, while she was still in town?" Neily asked because of the way her grandmother had made it sound.

Ruby nodded again, this time sadly. "I don't know for sure what happened, but, yes, even before I married your grandfather and left Northbridge for that time, Theresa and I…drifted apart, I suppose you could say."

"Why?" asked Wyatt.

"It was after her parents were killed. Hector Tyson—" Ruby paused. "You probably don't know who I'm talking about," she said to Wyatt.

"Actually, his name has already come up. I haven't met him."

"Well, Hector—who was…oh, I think eight or…no, nine years older than Theresa and I—Hector had inherited the lumberyard from his own father and he and Theresa's father were sort of business partners."

"How *sort of?*" Neily asked. Her grandmother was obviously giving them some background and Neily thought that they might as well have all the details just in case something provided an additional clue that could help Theresa now.

"Well, Theresa's father was a carpenter with ambitions to build houses, and Hector owned the lumberyard," Ruby explained. "It wasn't as if they'd formed a company, but they had dealings. Theresa's father had gone out on a financial limb to buy most of the land that sits just east of Main Street—from three blocks or so behind Main all the way out to where the Floyds' cornfields start—"

Neily knew Wyatt had no base of reference beyond Main Street, so she said, "That would be where the houses are that your grandmother said had all belonged to her father. The land Hector Tyson ended up selling off in lots."

"That's right," Ruby confirmed. "In those days, Theresa's father owned that land and it was *his* plan to sell the lots and design and construct the houses himself. Which of course Hector was in favor of, because he would have supplied all the materials. Theresa talked about how her father said he'd taken a big risk but he had so many plans and he was sure they were going to get rich."

"Had my great-grandfather set anything into motion before he died?" Wyatt asked.

"I don't think so. As far as I knew, it was all still in the talking or planning stages."

"And then Theresa's parents died," Neily said, again to be sure of the time line.

"Poor Theresa," Ruby sighed. "We were just girls, and all of a sudden she didn't have anyone…"

"She had you, didn't she?" Neily asked.

"She had me to cry with, to hold her hand, but what could I do other than that? She stayed at my house for a little while but…" Ruby looked shamefaced. "Times were hard. There had been a drought for two years running and my family only had what the farm brought in and what my father could earn doing odd jobs. Because of the drought the farm hadn't brought in much of anything. Everyone in Northbridge was struggling so they weren't hiring for odd jobs, and then that winter hit—one of the worst anyone had ever seen—and that just made things worse. Daddy couldn't afford another mouth to feed."

Neily recognized the helpless remorse in her grandmother. She'd seen it before on the rare occasions when Ruby had made any reference to Neily's father and the fact that there was nothing she could do to force him to return to or take care of the family he'd left behind.

Ruby went on, "Theresa moved in with us and she and I were just as close as always. But we couldn't have her stay and that was when Hector stepped in. He offered to have Theresa live with him and his wife."

Neily exchanged confused looks with Wyatt.

"We knew Hector ended up owning Gram's land, but she *lived* with him, too?" Wyatt asked as if he might have misunderstood.

"With him and his wife—Gloria. She was a pinch-faced woman who was five years older than Hector. No one ever understood *that* match—except that she came with a lot of money from a wealthy family in Denver. Still, everyone was surprised that he would settle for someone like her."

"Why?" Neily asked.

"You might not believe it to see him now, but in his day, Hector was as handsome as handsome could be. All the young girls in town had a little crush on him—me and Theresa included. He had wavy raven-black hair and the bluest eyes…and, oh, boy, did he know it! He was such a flirt…" Ruby smiled at Wyatt. "I'll bet you've done some of that yourself."

Neily glanced at Wyatt, worried that that might have made him uncomfortable. But he laughed it off and her grandmother went on.

"Anyway, to answer your question, Wyatt—yes, Theresa went to live with Hector and his wife. Your grandmother's only family was an aunt in Missoula, and the aunt had some kind of health problems right then so she couldn't have Theresa come to her."

Ruby sipped her coffee before she said, "Theresa and I both thought it was odd. Hector was saying that as a close friend and business partner of her father's, that he was like family and that Theresa should go live with him and his wife. They had a big house and they were better off than anybody else in town then—like I said, Gloria had come from money, and they didn't have any children—"

Wyatt interrupted, "And how old were they?"

"Hector would have been… Well, twenty-six because we were seventeen, so that would have made Gloria thirty-one. But the fact that they were fairly young was actually a factor—folks thought it might do Theresa some good to be with youthful people."

"But you and Theresa thought it was odd," Neily reminded her grandmother.

"Well, Hector *hadn't* really been a close friend of Theresa's father, and even though they had planned to do business, they weren't what you'd call business partners. And Hector and Gloria didn't seem like the kind of couple who would *want* to take someone in. So it seemed a little strange."

"But Gram still went to live with them?" Wyatt asked.

Ruby shrugged. "She didn't have a choice. All her own family's money was tied up in that land, so it wasn't as if there was cash to help out with her room and board—wherever she went to live, she *was* just another mouth to feed. It was awful all the way around."

The waitress came to refill their cups. When she had left, Wyatt summarized, "So Hector Tyson was her only option."

"That was what it came down to," Ruby said. "It wasn't as if he was a stranger or anything—no one in Northbridge was a stranger, and everyone said what a nice thing it was for him and Gloria to do. But then— to me at least—it seemed like the Tysons just cut Theresa off from everyone."

"Why was that?" Neily asked.

"I'm not saying that Theresa was a lighthearted girl all along—she wasn't," Ruby replied. "She was a quiet, melancholy sort of person even before her parents died. She was very sensitive and emotional and easily upset, and of course all of that got worse after she lost her mother and father, and even before she went to live with Hector and Gloria.

"But then Theresa moved in with the Tysons, and it felt to me like they'd taken her away to a castle, pulled up the drawbridge, and no one could get to her. Every time I tried to see her or call her, either Hector or Gloria would say Theresa was napping or that she had a headache or that she just wasn't up to having company or socializing. They said she was upset, that she was sick from grief. That she didn't *want* to be around me or anyone else. And maybe that was true—"

"But you didn't think so," Wyatt said.

Neily's grandmother shrugged again. "I don't know. I'd just never had Theresa *not* want to see me. I thought maybe she held it against me that I hadn't been able to make my parents let her stay with us. That maybe she was mad at me. But she didn't see anybody else, either. And she never came back to school—her folks died in mid-December, she was with my family and me through the holidays and then she went with Hector and Gloria. Like I said, that winter was a bad one—blizzard after blizzard. School didn't open again until the end of January and when it did, the Tysons said Theresa was too distraught to go to classes. And she never came back. She might have stayed in Northbridge, but she didn't end up finishing high school or graduating with the rest of us the way she'd wanted to."

"The Tysons kept her prisoner?" Wyatt asked, clearly getting alarmed at the thought.

"No," Ruby was quick to answer, apparently seeing his concern as well as Neily did. "I don't think it was like that. Maybe it was just the beginning of the problems she has now—from what little Neily told me before you got here, Wyatt, Theresa stays cooped up and doesn't want to be with most people, so maybe that was just when that started. Maybe she just pulled into herself and maybe Hector and Gloria weren't doing anything but what she wanted."

"But you aren't sure about that?" Wyatt persisted.

"I truly don't know. I know that on the rare occasions when Theresa would come out of their house either Hector or Gloria was always with her, and the minute anyone went near Theresa they would step in and insist on taking her home. Everyone was sure Theresa was just sunk in her grief over her parents and I'm sure she was, but the situation seemed off to me."

"It *is* pretty much what goes on now, though," Neily pointed out, feeling the need to since she could tell Wyatt was still up in arms over the things her grandmother was saying.

"You and Mary Pat run interference for Theresa," she said to Wyatt. "I did the same thing before you got here. Theresa didn't want to see anyone who was working on the house last week so I made sure she didn't have to."

"That's true," Wyatt conceded. "It's just that in the problems she's always had, the reclusiveness is the most recent—it hasn't *always* been a problem."

"But it's possible that she went through a bout of it then, that she improved, then sank back into it," Neily said. "That's how illnesses like your grandmother's can go. I'm not a fan of Hector Tyson, but you can't jump to the conclusion that he held Theresa *prisoner* based on this. He and his wife *could* have just been doing a good deed."

Wyatt smiled at her. "That's what I like about

you—you're always fair and willing to give the benefit of the doubt."

Neily wished that even the slightest compliment from him didn't please her as much as it did. But despite the serious nature of their conversation, Wyatt's effects on her were still so strong they were nearly palpable. And she couldn't wait to be alone with him again….

But she *wasn't* alone with him yet, so she pulled her gaze away from him to look at her grandmother.

"How long was Theresa with the Tysons?" she asked to get herself back on track.

"The whole rest of the time she was in Northbridge. I'd already left town when I heard through letters from other people that Theresa's aunt finally felt well enough to have her move there, and that she'd sold the land to Hector and that he was doing what her father had planned all along—selling it off and making money hand over fist. Everybody figured she'd sold the land so she could afford to leave and start a new life somewhere."

"And that was it? You didn't ever see or hear from her?" Neily said.

"After Pops was finished in the army and we went home to Northbridge I asked around about Theresa. I found out that she was paying to have the house looked after, that it was handled through some lawyer in Missoula. I got his address and wrote to her a few times in care of him. But if she got my letters she never answered them. I just thought she'd moved on with her life. It made me sad, but what could I do?"

"And now she's come back to Northbridge saying

she wants back what was taken from her," Neily told her grandmother. "We're wondering if she means the land."

"I heard that Hector paid about twenty-five cents on the dollar for what that land was worth—that was sort of a steal. But to me it doesn't seem quite right that Theresa would do something that must have been almost unthinkable for her—going back to Northbridge now—over land she sold fifty-some years ago. Even if she did make a bad deal with Hector, I wouldn't think it would matter so much to her, especially all these years later…"

They'd finished their second cups of coffee by then, and when a small van with the name of the complex printed on the side pulled up Ruby nodded toward it.

"I can catch that back to my building. Why don't I do that and you two can get going? I'm worried about you driving all the way to Northbridge in this storm."

Neily had intended to change clothes at her grandmother's apartment and get ready for her night on the town with Wyatt. But it was becoming increasingly clear that what Ruby said was true—they shouldn't put off the return trip. So, since she hadn't yet told Ruby about her plans, she didn't bother now.

Instead she and her grandmother exchanged some parting chitchat and made promises to call. Then Ruby told Wyatt how glad she was to meet him and asked him to say hello to his grandmother for her.

"I'd love it if she'd see me. I'd get up to Northbridge for that."

"I'll try to persuade her," Wyatt said.

Neily hugged her grandmother and Ruby left them alone just as the waitress was bringing their check.

"Did I overhear something about you trying to get somewhere north of here?" the waitress asked.

"Yes, to Northbridge," Neily answered.

"You don't want to do that. Highways in that direction are closing because of blowing snow. Police are trying to get help to a whole bunch of people stuck out there."

"Uh-oh," Neily said after the waitress had retreated.

"We're stuck?" Wyatt said as if it amused him.

"We can check with the highway patrol—maybe she's wrong."

"But probably not," he said with a glance out the window at the weather. "Do you want to run and catch your grandmother so you can stay with her?"

Neily shook her head. "We never stay with her. She only has one bedroom."

"What do you do if you don't make the visit a round-trip?"

"There's a motel nearby. Or a nicer hotel a little farther but still on the complex."

"Does the hotel have a restaurant?"

"I think so."

"So we might not be able to have exactly the night out I was picturing but we could get a couple of rooms and still have dinner at least."

There was actually a twinkle in his eyes that made Neily laugh. "Two rooms?" she said firmly.

"Absolutely," he assured her. "On different floors if it would make you feel better."

Neily looked out the window again as the driver helped her grandmother into the van with wind whipping snow all around them. It was no weather to be out in, that was for sure.

And the idea of a room in a hotel, a romantic dinner with Wyatt while Mother Nature wreaked havoc outside?

Neily could think of a whole lot worse ways to spend Sunday night.

Chapter Thirteen

The hotel Neily had mentioned to Wyatt, while nicer than the motel, was not the Ritz. But in the middle of a blizzard they couldn't be picky.

It was also swamped with guests who, like Neily and Wyatt, were stranded. By the time they arrived, all the single rooms were occupied and only suites were available. Their best option was a suite with a sitting room separating two bedrooms.

They purchased enough necessities at the gift shop to get by, but when they tried to make reservations at the restaurant, they were told that the hotel catered to the nearby senior residents on Sunday evening and served only a cafeteria-style buffet supper. The good news was that afterward there was live music and dancing in the lounge.

It was hardly a fancy night on the town, yet as Neily dressed for the evening she had no complaints. All she was thinking about was that she got to spend the time with Wyatt.

She changed into the dress she'd brought for tonight—a black minidress that skimmed her body and was scooped at the neckline to show a hint of cleavage. Thigh-high black nylons and heels completed the outfit, and she topped it off by brushing her hair to fall free and adding a smoky eyeshadow, a bit darker blush and a lipstick that guaranteed not to rub off.

Then she met Wyatt in the living-room-like area between their bedrooms.

He was wearing the same impeccably tailored navy-blue suit he'd worn to the wedding Friday night, this time with a blindingly white shirt and a yellow tie. The shirt turned his eyes to silver, and the tie brought out the sunstreaks in his hair. Neily didn't know if they were going to be overdressed but she didn't care. Wyatt looked more handsome than should have been legal, and the fact that his jaw dropped for a split second when he first saw her made it worth it even if they were.

Unfortunately the crowded hotel dining room was filled with weather-frazzled guests and talkative geriatrics who had been bussed in, which did not make for much privacy through dinner. With trays in hand, Neily and Wyatt couldn't find a free table. Just as they were about to take their food into the lobby, an elderly couple insisted that they join them. The meal ended up like a double date, during which they got to know all about Audie and Sheila Weinstein's sixty-three-year marriage.

The lounge was equally as full afterward but the lights were low, there was a roaring blaze in a fireplace along one wall, and the romantic ballads from the forties and fifties being sung by a rotund woman with piano accompaniment finally made it seem more like a night on the town. A night for much older people, but still a night on the town.

And when Wyatt took her out onto the dance floor, Neily was actually glad not to be in a louder, trendier club with him.

But while what she would have liked was to just lay her cheek to his chest and absorb the feel of him, she knew she shouldn't do that. So she finally opted for the conversation she'd intended to have over dinner.

"I've been thinking about that comment my grandmother made at the end today," Neily said as they danced. "About how she didn't think your grandmother would be as intent as she is to get something back if that something was only land. The same thing has crossed my mind. I even asked Cheryl if there was any jewelry missing— anything that might have more sentimental value."

"Nothing is that I know of," Wyatt said, expertly twirling Neily, then pulling her back into his arms.

"Or that anyone else knows of, according to Cheryl," Neily added. "But more and more I'm thinking that it just doesn't feel like *land* is the reason Theresa has come back to Northbridge."

"What *do* you think she came to get back?"

"I don't know. Something more personal. More important to her. Something so important that she hasn't been able to let go of it all these years."

"Mmm," Wyatt conceded. "You could be right." Then he smiled a small, faraway smile and said, "I really do love my grandmother."

"I know you do," Neily said, confused by where that had come from.

"And I liked your grandmother today, too. I thought she was great."

"She is," Neily agreed, not understanding where that had come from, either.

"And Sheila and Audie Weinstein? Nice people to invite us to share their table, interesting dinner companions, and look at 'em go over there—they can really dance…"

Neily scanned the crowded floor until she spotted the elderly couple. Wyatt was right, they were like two pros. But still she had no idea why they were talking about this, and so she merely said, "Uh-huh."

"But tonight I wanted to just be with you. In the here and now. Not in your past or mine, or my grandmother's or your grandmother's, or even the Weinsteins'. I want to just enjoy this—" His arm tightened around her waist. "So what do you say?"

Neily laughed. "Okay."

"So no more talk of days-gone-by, or of geriatric issues, or even of my grandmother?"

Neily smiled. "I think I can do that."

The song ended, the dancing stopped so everyone could applaud the singer, and then, when the singer started another set, Wyatt took Neily back into his arms to go on dancing.

This time he initiated the conversation. "What would you think of having a Home-Max in Northbridge?"

That surprised her. "Seriously?"

"I've been thinking about it this week, I've done some looking around, had some numbers crunched, and I talked to Marti and Ry while you were getting dressed tonight. We wouldn't open one of the bigger stores, but we've done a few smaller versions here and there, and I think Northbridge might be a decent market for one of those. What do you think?"

"That Hector Tyson will hate you and do everything he can to make it difficult for you. But I also think it would be great."

Especially since it seemed as if it could make Wyatt a fixture in Northbridge.

But just when she was thinking about that and about how much she liked the idea, he said, "My sister, Marti, is coming into Northbridge tomorrow."

"To see you guys or to stay?"

"To stay with Gram and Mary Pat while I head back to Missoula."

That hit Neily like a ton of bricks. "You're leaving?"

"It's how it will go for now—Marti, Ry and I will take turns with Gram and do what work we can from Northbridge while the other two do what we always do in Missoula—"

"So you're leaving for two weeks?"

"At least. Depending on what any of us has going on, it could vary. All I know for sure is that Marti is coming in tomorrow, she'll shop for a location for the new store and look after Gram, and I need to leave for Missoula."

His being in Northbridge had never been permanent, Neily reminded herself. She should have seen this coming. Been prepared.

But somehow she hadn't. And wasn't.

All she said, though, was "Oh."

And just that quick tonight became all the more precious.

"I think you'll like Marti," Wyatt was saying as if his sister wasn't the last thing on Neily's mind. "She's going through a rough time right now and we're hoping Northbridge will do her some good, too."

Neily knew she should probably ask more about that but she was having too much trouble accepting that Wyatt was leaving soon. That she wouldn't be seeing him every day the way she had since he'd come to town.

"Will you show her around a little?" he asked. "Maybe give her your opinion on where a prime place for a store would be? Make her feel at home the way you have me?"

Direct questions—he was asking her direct questions that he expected her to answer…

"Sure," she said, only partially aware of what she was agreeing to.

"Noah Perry starts work on the remodel tomorrow, too," he said then. "We'll all be overseeing that, so hopefully I can introduce them before I leave—"

"You know how you don't want to talk about the past and the grandmothers and the geriatrics?" Neily heard herself say in pure reflex because she didn't think she could bear to hear him say *leave* one more time.

"Uh-huh?"

"Well, I'd like it if we didn't have to talk about you going back to Missoula right now, too."

Wyatt smiled down at her with that twinkle in his eye again. "Because you can't stand the thought?" he asked as if it delighted him.

"Because we're supposed to be staying in the here and now tonight, remember?"

"And because you can't stand the thought," he added conclusively.

"Why wouldn't I be able to stand the thought?" she bluffed airily. "You'll be back."

"Yeah, I will be," he said in a reassuring tone.

It didn't help and about the only thing that did was when he pulled her closer and held her tighter.

From then on neither of them said much of anything. They exchanged a little small talk but for the most part they let the music do the talking for them.

After a while Neily's head *was* on Wyatt's chest, and his chin was resting on top. He was keeping their clasped hands close between them, and unlike the Weinsteins they were barely dancing at all, but merely swaying together in one place.

They made it through every dance that way. Even as it got later and later, as the floor began to clear, as the senior bus took Audie and Sheila and the rest of their neighbors home. Then the singer announced her last song and that the lounge would be closing, and still it seemed to Neily that she hadn't had enough time in Wyatt's arms.

He held her hand as they went up to their suite and with each of the six floors the elevator took them past Neily's anticipation rose, too. After all, they were on their way up to a hotel room. Just the two of them. And if tonight was anything like the last few…

But once Wyatt had her behind the closed doors of their suite he let go of her hand, took her by the shoulders and kissed only her forehead.

Neily looked up at him and apparently he could see in her face that she had been expecting more because he shook his head.

"This place is a lot riskier than your playroom," he decreed. "Anything that gets started here will get finished here. And I won't have you thinking I took advantage of the situation."

No, go ahead, take advantage, she almost said.

But then she thought about the previous night in the playroom, and how she'd stopped him from going any further than they had.

I'm the one who said no, that it wasn't the best idea…

And tonight she was also thinking about him leaving Northbridge, about how she wasn't sure when she would see him again once he did. And if, after he left town, they only saw each other on rare occasions, when their paths just happened to cross or in the course of her working with Theresa, wouldn't it be awkward and uncomfortable and embarrassing if they'd slept together this one time?

Which probably made it an even worse idea tonight.

No matter how much she might be wanting it...

So she nodded and said, "You promised two rooms, we have two rooms, we should use two rooms," as if she were in complete agreement.

Wyatt nodded in the direction of hers. "Go on, get some sleep."

"You, too," she said, even though he was still holding on to her shoulders and neither of them had moved an inch.

Wyatt's silvery eyes studied her face for a moment and she knew he was fighting not to kiss her the kind of kiss that had kicked things off the night before. But he didn't. He squeezed her shoulders and then took his hands away.

"Go. Run for cover," he whispered, joking.

She knew that if she didn't put a safe distance between them right away then his will wouldn't be strong enough to last.

So she called upon her own willpower again and said, "I'll see you in the morning." Then she turned and went into her room.

Where she closed the door, undressed, and put on the top to the set of red silk pajamas that Wyatt had bought at the gift shop for them to split up.

But when all of that was done and she stood at the foot of her double bed telling herself to get into it, she couldn't do it.

All she could think about—all she'd thought about

since the minute she'd come into this room—was Wyatt. And how this could be her last chance, her only chance, to have a night with him.

She told herself that this wasn't an impulse or a heat-of-the-moment decision—well, not completely—because it wasn't as if she were blinded by his kisses or by his hands on her.

Yes, she wanted him as much as if that were the case. But she also wanted this night with him even if there were never any others. Even if she did have to face him again, maybe work with him again, even if it might be embarrassing or awkward or uncomfortable later on. Even if the fact that he was leaving Northbridge did make it a potentially worse idea than it had seemed before, it also made her want even more not to miss this one opportunity....

She pivoted on her heels, went out the door, across the living room and raised her fist to knock.

Be sure, she told herself before she did.

But she was sure. She was sure that she wanted him. No matter what.

She knocked.

The door opened.

And there was Wyatt, wearing only the pajama bottoms, his flat belly, his narrow waist, his broad chest and massive shoulders bare for her to see and every bit as beautiful as she'd thought they might be.

Now that they were face-to-face she didn't know what to say.

But she didn't have to say anything because Wyatt

smiled knowingly, took her hand and brought her into his room and into his arms in one smooth move without the need for either of them to speak.

He cupped her face in both hands to tilt it so he could find her mouth with his in a kiss that was more like what she'd expected when they'd returned to the suite. His lips parted, her lips parted, and his tongue didn't hesitate to make itself known.

Neily raised her hands to his chest, letting the warmth of him seep through her palms, learning the texture of his skin and how solid was the wall of muscle it encased.

And if she'd had the slightest doubt about this, it left her then because nothing had ever felt as right as being there with him did.

His hands went into her hair, cushioning her head as he took the kiss to a new level, opening his mouth wider, the play of his tongue insistent now.

But Neily met and matched him, not shy or timid but willing and eager to cast aside all inhibitions.

While their mouths went on plundering, his hands began a steady descent to her shoulders again, to her arms, to the top button of the pajama top.

He paused there a moment, but if he thought she might stop him he learned otherwise when Neily ran her own hands around to his back instead.

His kiss turned instantly hungrier as he unfastened the buttons, letting the pajama top fall open.

In went his hands, to breasts that were already eager for his touch, already tight and straining at the tips for more of what they'd had so little of the previous night.

Great hands—big, strong, adept, they kneaded and massaged, toyed and teased. Fingertips plucked her nipples, gently tugged at them, pulled and pressed and turned them to diamonds while his mouth feasted on hers.

Wyatt abandoned her breasts then, though, wrapping her in his arms to spin her around, nearer to the bed where he eased her to lie flat on her back and stretched out alongside of her.

His mouth pulled away while his tongue alone did the ravaging of her lips, her teeth, her own tongue, teasing and tantalizing her.

He braced himself on one arm and sent his free hand to explore again. But rather than returning to her breasts he cupped her hip instead, slipping a single finger under the strip of lace at the side of her bikini pants.

Then his mouth left hers completely, trailing a path of kisses to the hollow of her throat, to the dip between her breasts and finally to her breast itself. But only to her nipple, where he placed the lightest kiss of all to the very crest.

Neily couldn't help the tiny groan that escaped her just before he took that nipple between his lips, pulling it in only slightly, then a bit farther, a bit stronger, farther and stronger until the torment had her spine arched off the mattress and both nipples so hard they ached.

She felt him smile, she felt his mouth lazily open against her flesh, his breath a gust of heat just before he encompassed her with that hot cove and began to work a magic she hadn't even imagined.

Her own hands were on him, on his back, on his sides. His stomach was flat and solid. He tensed as if he were ticklish when her hand grazed his side. And his rear end was taut and tight beneath the silk when she ventured with her hands where only her eyes had gone before.

The hardness of him made itself known at her hip, and as terrific as he'd looked in those pajama bottoms when he'd opened the bedroom door, now all she wanted was to be rid of them. And if there were no other advantages to silk, the one she discovered then was that they slid right off.

He wasn't wearing anything underneath them and after kicking them out of the way, Wyatt was stark naked beside her.

Desperate to see him, she rolled to her side. It cost her his mouth at her breast because he came up for air, but the sight was worth it—male perfection, that's what he was, with long, thick proof of just how much he wanted her there for her to see and savor.

She reached for him, grasping that iron-hard shaft, claiming it and making him moan before he nearly tore her panties off and gave a little back with a hand that went exploring between her legs while his mouth returned to her other breast, giving it equal time and attention.

It was his finger that gave the preview then, slipping into her and drawing out, again and again until Neily wasn't sure she could last another second.

But just as that thought flashed through her, Wyatt rolled away, reached into the bedside drawer and returned with protection.

"The gift shop. Just in case. I thought I was going to end up leaving them for the next guy."

Neily laughed and kissed him, trailing her hands all over his body as he sheathed himself.

When he had he lay flat on his back.

"I want to see you," he said, pulling her to straddle him, guiding her with hands on her hips to come down over that massive shaft until they were fitted together as if they were meant to be one.

She still had on the pajama top and he left it, reaching to her breasts again, studying her with eyes that bathed her in admiration, keeping both of their lower bodies still and just staying there inside of her, making it his home.

He deserted one breast to clamp that hand behind her neck to pull her down far enough to kiss him, returning it to her breast when he had what he wanted. Then both hands slid down from there, to her sides and farther until his thumbs had reached the very juncture of her thighs, touching her in a way no one ever had before.

Neily's mouth over his just opened as the breath went out of her, and that was when he started to move, using those big hands on her hips to hold her to each thrust while his thumbs still kept the most tender of pressures. Up and down, deeper into her, then less, deeper and away…

She knew he was watching but she didn't care and she couldn't keep her own eyes open any longer as he took her higher and higher to a peak more potent, more powerful than anything she'd ever known. Her whole body stiffened and when it did he took his thumbs away, pressed in on her thighs and held her tight and firm around him, plunging even more deeply into her as wave after wave after wave went through her, carrying her with it, leaving her naked breasts heaving between the curtains of the red silk that had fallen off one shoulder, every breath a new beginning until that most incredible of crests finally began to recede.

That was when Wyatt wrapped his arms around her—one around her back, one around her rear—and rolled her so she was lying flat and he was on top of her, cradled in her open legs. His hands were on either side of her head, his elbows were locked, and he held himself braced above her while he plunged even more deeply into her than she'd known was possible. Thrusting and retreating, again and again.

She drank in the view of that chiseled face, of those sinewy arms and shoulders, of that carved and honed chest as he raced to his own climax and finally found it, in a glorious release that set off an aftershock in her that took her by surprise.

Then slowly, slowly, it all ebbed and he exhaled a long, replete breath. Relaxing inch by inch, he lowered himself to kiss her again, a kiss that was raw and primal and as intimate a connection as those other parts of their bodies that were still joined.

And then they weren't, and when that kiss ended he flipped over onto his back and brought her to lie against his side, both arms around her to hold her firmly.

"No question about it, this is my favorite blizzard *ever*," he said in a playful, ragged voice.

"Mine, too," Neily confessed, unable to keep a little awe from her own tone.

"I'm thinking a nap and then we try out your bed."

She laughed. "Okay," she agreed, already hoping the nap didn't take too long.

Wyatt's arms tightened around her. He kissed the top of her head, and she felt him losing the battle with sleep. So she closed her eyes and gave in to her own weariness.

But, oh, it felt good to lie there against him, held by his strong arms, her body aching for more even though he'd left her satisfied beyond her wildest dreams.

And even though she knew it wasn't possible, as she drifted off to sleep herself she couldn't help making a silent wish: that the snow would go on forever and they'd never have to leave that suite.

Chapter Fourteen

By noon on Monday the spring blizzard had stopped, the sun was out, and the highway back to Northbridge was open again.

After a night with very little sleep, Neily was out like a light in the passenger seat of Wyatt's SUV. Wyatt was feeling the effects of too little rest himself, but he wasn't having any trouble staying awake to drive. Not when he had so many things on his mind.

He took his eyes off the road long enough to glance over at Neily just because he wanted a look at her.

Her head was propped against the window. Her long, thick eyelashes were dark against the peaches-and-cream of her flawless skin. Her lips were just the slightest bit slack—soft, sweet lips that he'd had all over him at one point or another the night before. And for two cents Wyatt would have pulled to the side of the highway and kissed her awake the way he had twice during the night and again this morning.

But the SUV didn't offer much privacy, so he fought the urge.

Even though it wasn't easy. Not when he wanted her even more now than he had before she'd shown up at his hotel-room door.

Which was part of what was keeping him wide awake.

When he'd made his decision not to get involved with anyone after Mikayla's death he hadn't only been determined not to, he'd also been convinced that he wouldn't ever feel this way about anyone again. And since then he hadn't met anyone who had gotten to him in the slightest, so he'd felt fairly safe.

Then he'd met Neily. And discovered there was a hole in his safety net because she *had* gotten to him.

Was it the vague resemblance to Mikayla? he asked himself, glancing again at Neily.

No, he really didn't see Mikayla in her at all now. Neily was calm and even-keeled where Mikayla had been high-strung. Neily was a small-town girl-next-door where Mikayla had been a hundred percent city girl. Neily was traditional; Mikayla had been all contemporary. And even when it came to family they were worlds apart—Neily was all about her sister and brothers, all about the people she cared for as a social worker, where Mikayla had had only a distant relationship with her own family.

So similarity didn't explain why—in just the blink of an eye—he was finding himself in this position.

About the only real similarity between the two of them was that they both made him happy.

Because Mikayla *had* made him happy, and now Neily did, too.

Which was tough.

Not that being happy was tough. It felt great. *He* felt great. Better than he'd thought he would ever feel again. And that was all because of Neily. Because she was fun and good-natured. Because she was understanding and compassionate and giving. Because behind that girl-next-door exterior was a simmering sexuality that he couldn't resist. And altogether it had absolutely gotten to him.

But now that that had happened, how could he go back to that plan to protect himself by *not* getting too close to anyone again? That plan not to put himself in a position where he cared for someone and lost them?

By remembering how bad it had been—hadn't that been what he'd told himself to do? To recall what it had been like after Mikayla and the baby had died. To relive those horrible black days and nights. The depression. The despair. The fear that it would never end. That he would never be able to get out of the pits…

Yeah, it had been bad…

And he knew he didn't want to do anything that could ever put him anywhere near that again.

But he also didn't want to go on without Neily. Without knowing more of what he had since he'd met her. More of what they'd shared last night.

So now what? he asked himself. Now what…?

Neily sighed in her sleep just then, and he had to look over at her once more. He just had to. He'd heard that same sigh a time or two during the night—when he'd touched her a certain way, when he'd satisfied her, just before she'd dozed off after this morning's round…

What the hell was he going to do, deny himself more of that?

Just thinking about it, imagining himself dropping her at her house, leaving Northbridge, going on without her, made him relive a portion of those dark, grieving days.

Only it wouldn't be fate that had snatched away his happiness. He'd be turning his back on it himself.

But what if he *didn't* turn his back on what had begun with Neily, what if he gave in to what he wanted, and *then* lost her somehow? It wouldn't be any easier than losing Mikayla had been. And he'd genuinely be back in the pits he might not make it out of again…

He took a deep breath and sighed, too, but his sigh sounded full of frustration.

What it came down to, he guessed, was what was more important to him—not risking his sanity or having Neily?

Some things she had said to him popped into his mind in answer to that. Things she'd said to him when he'd told her this was something he worried about, something he thought he *needed* to worry about.

Neily had said his grandmother's condition was an illness. She'd said that his ability to come out of his own grief was proof that he *hadn't* inherited the illness.

Was she right? he wondered now. Could she be right?

His grandmother's bouts with depression had tracked throughout her life. And according to Neily's grandmother, it hadn't even been just in response to the death of his great-grandparents. Ruby had said that his grandmother had always been a melancholy, introspective, overly sensitive person who was easily upset. None of that had ever described *him.*

So maybe there wasn't any reason to believe that another loss would send him over the edge.

Yet he wasn't fooling himself. He knew that when he committed himself to someone he went all the way, and not having that work out would hit him hard no matter what. So it wasn't anything he would ever want or invite. It was something he would do everything possible to avoid. But could he weather it again if he let this go any further with Neily and lost her?

No, he wouldn't want to, but when he thought about it, he thought he could. After all, wasn't that what he'd told his sister not long ago? That her grief would pass? That regardless of how bad it was, it did get better, it did go away? He'd said it because it had all been true for him. And if it had been true once, it could be true again.

So Neily was right—there was a difference between grief and what his grandmother suffered. Finally realizing that, believing it, made him feel as if an enormous weight had been lifted off his shoulders.

And without that weight holding him back, keeping him from going on with his life, why *couldn't* he go on with it?

His gaze was drawn back to Neily, the woman who had helped open his eyes. The woman whom he'd been so attracted to right from the start that not even his fears and all the issues that had come from them had let him resist her sweetness, her kindness, her humor. The woman who had pulled him that last mile back into the land of the living with her understanding, with her sense of fun, with so much warmth and appeal, with that just-below-the-surface sensuality peeking out at him.

He couldn't see any reason why he *couldn't* go on with his life now, and Neily was the woman he wanted with him to do that. He knew that as surely as he'd ever known anything. Neily was the woman he wanted to spend the rest of his life with....

"Wow," he whispered.

The Northbridge city limits sign came into view at that moment and Wyatt did pull off the road then, parking on the shoulder as close as he could get to the bank of snow the plows had left. He left the engine idling, turning partially in his seat so he could look at Neily once more as she slept against the window. Only this time all he could do was smile.

It was as if a dense fog had been lifted from around him and in the clearing was this wonderful, beautiful woman he wanted to spend the rest of his days with. No matter what. Being with her was worth anything—everything.

That was something he never thought he'd feel again as long as he lived.

And now that he did, he couldn't wait to tell her.

* * *

Neily woke up when the SUV stopped. She opened her eyes and turned away from the window to sit straight in her seat.

She glanced over and discovered that Wyatt was watching her. "Haven't they cleared the road into town yet?"

"I'm sure they have."

Neily looked outside and all around them. "What's wrong then?"

Wyatt shook his head and smiled bigger. "Not a thing. I've just been thinking and I didn't want to get all the way back without telling you that you were right."

"Well, of course I am," she joked as if she knew what he was talking about. "But just because I've been asleep for a while and might not be at the top of my game—what am I right about?"

"Me."

That didn't clear things up.

"Okay…"

"For the first time I've been thinking about your theory—"

"I have a lot of theories. Which one in particular?"

"The one about my fears that the rough patch I went through after Mikayla and the baby died was a sign that I could lapse into the same problems my grandmother has."

"Oh, that one," Neily said. "I'm glad you can finally see it." She thought that the fact that he couldn't wait to tell her showed what a relief it was to him.

Wyatt went on. "I also realized that if I ever had to suffer another loss, I could get through that, too."

"Because you have the resiliency your grandmother doesn't," Neily confirmed.

"And that set me free," he announced momentously.

Neily smiled. "Freedom suits you," she said because he looked energized. His eyes were an even more sparkling silver-blue and no one would ever have guessed that he was as sleep deprived as she knew he was.

"Free to move on and start over," he added. "To have what I want, what I've always wanted, what I want again—which is to be married and to have a family. And I want it with you."

She hadn't seen *that* coming—and it jarred her.

But Wyatt didn't wait for her to say anything. He merely continued. "I thought I could never have the same thing I had with Mikayla—and not only did I think I couldn't *risk* being in as deep as I was with her, I didn't think I was even capable of feeling the same things. But here you are and…" He sighed, he chuckled, he shook his head. "I'm in. Just like that. I'm in head-over-heels—more, even, than I was with Mikayla. And I won't let anything stand in the way of you and I having what I had with her."

For a moment Neily wondered if she was understanding him. If she was still half asleep or too tired to grasp what he was telling her. But regardless, it was setting off alarms in her.

"You mean you want to just…restore your life the

way you've hired Noah to restore your grandmother's house?" she asked.

"I guess I do feel a little like my life has been restored. I've spent the last two years since Mikayla died thinking that being married, having kids—that whole thing—was just over for me. Forever. That I had to be grateful that I came out of the hell of grief and not rock the boat from here on by trying again. But now…yeah, you could say that the vision I had of my future has been restored to me."

Neily could feel her head shaking even before she said, "And I'm just the way to pick up where you left off?"

That squashed his smile. "No, you're not *just* the way to pick up where I left off."

But she thought otherwise.

"It's tough," she told him. "I'm right here, invested in this, and I know I'm a completely different person from your late wife. But I'm not sure you see that. I think you've given yourself permission to have what you once had before, and I'm just someone with the right hair color to be the missing piece that puts you on that track again."

"The way you fit the bill for that Trent guy to mold into his image of the perfect wife?" Wyatt finished. "No, that's not it at all! I can give you a long list of how you're different from Mikayla and there's no way I'd change a single thing about you to make you more like her. Mikayla was Mikayla, you're you—"

"But you still had a happy marriage that you want to have again, only with me as the wife. I'd still be filling someone else's shoes. I'd be the understudy sent on stage when the person who'd really won the role couldn't go on. With Trent I had to try to fit some imaginary picture he had, with you I'd have to—"

"You'd have to just be yourself," Wyatt cut her off firmly.

Neily stared at him, wondering if she could trust that. Wishing she could.

But her own imagination began to weave a scenario. A scenario in which she was his wife when to him *wife* still might mean Mikayla. If she didn't do something the way Mikayla had done it—the way he'd liked it done— wouldn't she come up short? If she asked something of him, needed something of him that Mikayla wouldn't have asked or needed, wouldn't she fail by comparison? If she wasn't as exciting, as unique, as original, wouldn't she seem boring or mundane or tedious?

And ultimately, would it be so different from what had happened with Trent? No, she might not be left trying to fulfill some fantasy or someone else's compulsive need for perfection, but wouldn't she always wonder and worry that she wasn't exactly what Wyatt had had before? What he wanted again? What he expected and hoped that she would be? Wasn't she likely to fall into the trap of trying to be what he seemed to want rather than merely who she was…?

"I wish we could have a future together," she heard herself say quietly, sadly. "But I don't think what you want is the future so much as it is to re-create the life that was taken from you."

"You mean like my grandmother?" he said in disbelief.

Neily merely shrugged her concession to that.

She'd never seen signs of a temper in him but she could tell he wasn't happy with her. His eyebrows were drawn into a *V* over the bridge of his nose and his eyes had lost their blue cast to turn the color of steel.

"So you lied," he accused. "You really do think I'm as emotionally messed up as my grandmother is."

"That's not what I said," she insisted.

"Sure, it is," he challenged. "In her way, my grandmother has been stuck in the past—obviously she hasn't been able to let go of it if decades later she was driven to get back to Northbridge at any cost, to do whatever it is she's doing here in order to *reclaim* something she thinks was taken from her. Now you're saying the same thing about me."

"I'm not saying the same thing about you—"

"Close enough," he decreed. "And for all we know, that's what's caused my grandmother's mental problems and depression—not being able to let go of the past, holding on to some idea, some obsession to get something back. My wife, my baby, my marriage and the life I thought I'd have were taken from me and now you're accusing me of trying to get it all back. Of using you to do it. And if that were true, I wouldn't be in any better shape than my grandmother is."

Neily was sleep deprived, too, despite her brief nap. She knew she wasn't thinking completely clearly, but she honestly hadn't intended to say that he was anything like Theresa.

Again, though, before she could mount her own

defense, he went on. "Do you honestly think that's what I want for myself? To hang on that desperately to the past? Do you think that for even a second I believe that trying to regain anything the way my grandmother thinks she can is what would make me happy? Or make what happened before okay or better somehow? Because that *would* be crazy."

He shook his head much the way she had moments earlier, only with some disgust. "It's ironic, isn't it? I just figured out that I *don't* have to worry about being as unstable as my grandmother, only to find out that no matter what you said, you think I am."

"I don't," Neily claimed. Even if she was also having problems trusting that he wasn't trying to reconstruct what he'd lost.

He shook his head again. "I want you, Neily," he said definitively. "I want whatever kind of future we can build together and I know damn good and well that it won't be like what I had before. That's okay. That's better. I'm not looking to recapture anything. I'm looking to start again. To start fresh."

But was he? Neily was too afraid that he might not be.

"If that's true then you'll find someone else," she said with a giant lump in her throat. "Someone who doesn't remind you or anyone else of Mikayla, so you'll know for sure—"

"I know for sure *now,* damn it!"

"But I don't," she said very, very softly. "Now can you please just take me home?"

"Tell me what to do to convince you?" he demanded.

Neily took another turn at shaking her head but she couldn't say more than a whispered, "Just take me home," because her throat was too clogged and she was fighting too hard not to cry.

Wyatt sighed, then shoved the SUV into gear and pulled onto the highway.

Neither of them said anything along the way. Neily was struggling not to break down in front of him and she thought he was too angry and frustrated with her to speak.

But when he pulled into her driveway he turned to her and said again, "Neily, please—tell me what to do to convince you?"

Neily could only shake her head yet again as she got out of his SUV and ran for her house.

But even as she let herself in she was beginning to wonder if she'd just made the wisest and most healthy decision she'd ever made—or the biggest mistake of her life.

Chapter Fifteen

"*This is Marti Grayson. I'm sorry to bother you this late but my grandmother is having a really bad time. We were hoping maybe you could come over…*"

After receiving Marti's late-night call, Neily had thrown on her jeans and hoodie, jumped in her car and was on her way to the old Hobbs house by 11:30 p.m.

I'm a wreck, Theresa is a wreck. Maybe there's something in the air, she thought as she raced the short distance between her place and Theresa's.

Neily hadn't been out since Wyatt had dropped her off that afternoon. She'd spent the rest of the day and evening pacing, crying, feeling about as awful as it was possible to feel. She could only hope that if Wyatt's sister had come into town, that meant he'd left for

Missoula. Because if she had to see him again right now, she didn't know how strong she could be. Especially when she'd had so many second thoughts as she'd rehashed their argument a million times in her mind...

Then she drove up to the Hobbs house and saw Wyatt's SUV parked in the driveway.

Neily's heart seemed to lodge in her throat, and for a moment she wondered if his sister's call had been a ploy to get her there.

But Marti Grayson had sounded genuinely frazzled, and if Theresa really was in trouble, Neily knew she couldn't turn around and go home.

Just focus on Theresa. Don't think about anything else, she told herself as she got out of her car.

Mary Pat was watching for her and opened the front door the minute Neily headed for the house.

"She's in a terrible way," the nurse said of Theresa as Neily rushed up the porch steps. "Even with her medication she's still agitated."

"What happened to set her off?" Neily asked as she reached Mary Pat.

Theresa's caregiver shrugged helplessly. "A nightmare, I think. She was sound asleep, woke up with a shriek, and she's been this way ever since."

"Is she in her room?" Neily asked when she'd gone in and Mary Pat was closing the door behind her.

"They have her in the sunroom."

With the nurse following her, Neily hurried to the sunroom. Wyatt and a woman who bore enough resemblance to him to make it obvious that she was his sister were trying to calm Theresa. But much like Neily had done all day, the elderly woman was pacing frantically.

"Hi, Theresa," Neily said as she went into the sunroom, not even casting a glance at Wyatt but much, much more aware of him than she wanted to be.

"Neily! Thank heaven! You'll do it for me, won't you? You'll get it back!" Theresa said desperately, charging to Neily to grasp both of her hands.

Neily thought it was at least a good sign that Theresa knew who she was. "Why don't we sit down?" she suggested in a soft, calm voice.

Theresa ignored the idea. "It came again in my sleep!" she said. "The cries. Those tiny little cries! They're far away but they're cries for me. I just know it."

"Sit down and tell me about it," Neily tried again.

But once more the older woman didn't seem to even register what Neily had said.

"Please! Tell me you'll help me," Theresa pleaded.

"You know I'll do everything I can," Neily assured her. "We're all here to help you."

"I can't stand the cries," Theresa said, sobbing herself now.

"Who's crying in your dream, Theresa?" Neily asked.

"You know," the older woman whispered. Then, glancing in the direction of her grandchildren, she said, "I can't say, but you know!"

Except that Neily *didn't* know. "Is it you who's crying or someone else?"

"I cried, too. I cried and cried."

"Over your family? Over selling the land?"

"Land?" Theresa shouted as if that had been the most ridiculous thing of all to think. "Land is nothing!"

"So in the dream you're crying for your family?"

"For what Hector took," Theresa moaned.

"But Hector didn't have anything to do with you losing your mother and father," Neily reasoned.

"He took what he gave to me. He gave it to me, Neily, and then, just when it would have been mine, he took it away! But I want it back. I *have* to have it back! That's the only thing that will stop the crying. You have to help me. You can do those things, you can make Hector tell you what he did with it so we can get it back," Theresa said.

But the longer she'd gone on speaking, the more she began to slur her words, the more droopy her eyelids became, and Neily could tell that whatever medication Mary Pat had given her had finally kicked in.

Then Theresa wilted and veered backward as if she'd lost her balance.

Neily tightened the hold she still had on Theresa's hands, and Marti—who was nearest—lunged for Theresa, too, to keep her on her feet.

"Will you go back to bed now, Gram?" the other woman asked gently.

Theresa seemed to be steadied but was becoming more loggy by the minute. "What if the dream comes again? The cries are so hard for me to hear…"

"Mary Pat and I will sit with you until you doze off again, and I'll sleep in your room with you—will that make you feel better?"

Theresa nodded as if she didn't have the strength for

more than that. Mary Pat stepped in so that she and Marti Grayson were on either side of Theresa, and they moved her in the direction of the sunroom door.

Then they were gone, and just that fast Neily was alone with Wyatt.

And *she* wanted to cry…

She didn't, but she also couldn't just turn around and run the way she wanted to. She had to be mature about this. And she had to look at him…

The women of the household had all been in bathrobes, but Wyatt had on a pair of low-riding jeans and a plain white T-shirt that hugged his magnificent torso like another skin. His hair appeared to have been combed with his fingers and the stubble that shadowed his face gave him a scruffy sexiness.

Neily swallowed the desire to just walk over to him without saying a word, wrap her arms around him and lay her head to his chest the way she had when they'd danced the night before. Instead she opted for trying to act as if they'd never shared anything that didn't have to do with his grandmother.

"Did that happen often before she came back here?" she asked somberly.

She saw him hesitate and she knew he was weighing whether or not to play this let's-pretend-nothing-else-is-going-on game. But in the end he conceded because with some reluctance he said, "She has nightmares, yeah. But this is the first time I've heard this version."

"And it's impossible to tell if there's any truth or reality to it," Neily said. "But if there is… Maybe I shouldn't say this but the way she made it sound, I kept thinking she might be talking about—"

"A baby," Wyatt said.

"Do you think…" Neily hated to even put any more of this into words.

But Wyatt wasn't so skittish. "That it could be a baby Hector gave her and then took away? I don't know. She *was* with him for eleven months."

"Oh, that would have been bad," Neily said as all the ramifications of something like that began to hit her.

"I thought it was rotten enough that maybe Hector had isolated her to con her out of her land. But if he seduced her—a grieving teenage girl who had had a crush on him—got her pregnant, somehow *took* the baby from her at some point…"

"It could have scarred her for life," Neily said softly.

"But it would make more sense than being this tormented over selling land." Wyatt paused and then, very pointedly, he added, "It's the *people* we lose—not the *things*—that pack the wallop."

Somehow Neily knew he wasn't talking solely about his grandmother. Or even referring to the loss of his wife and baby. That she was who he was talking about losing now.

"I can't…" Neily shook her head. "I can't think about this anymore tonight." Not about something having happened to Theresa that could have been even worse than they'd assumed up to that point, and not about her own decisions today. "I should go," she said in a near panic.

Wyatt shrugged. "Okay."

The ease with which he agreed shocked her.

Then he added, "But I'm not."

Confused, Neily stared at him. "You're not what?" she asked dimly.

"Going to go. I'm not leaving Northbridge."

No! He couldn't stay! She'd been worried she wasn't strong enough to resist him if she had to see him tonight. How could she be strong enough to resist him if she saw him all the time?

But she couldn't let him know what was going through her mind, so she fought to maintain some composure and said, "Why would you stay here?"

"Gram wants to, and since Marti and Ry agree that we should open a Home-Max here, I decided to relocate. To move to Northbridge permanently and commute to Missoula when I need to. I decided," he said, speaking slowly, patiently, "that I'm not giving up on you. That I won't fault you for not being impulsive enough to jump in with both feet right now, and that I'm going to take my time showing you that I honestly do want a new life and a fresh start. With you."

Neily just stared at him, letting that sink in.

She'd realized during her marathon day of misery that her need to deny herself a future with him was more about her, about how she'd compromised herself to fit Trent's fantasies of perfection and worked so hard to fulfill them. That this was about how *she* didn't want to slip into something like that with Wyatt—because even if it *wasn't* what he was looking for, she was afraid it was something she'd feel compelled to do anyway.

And she didn't want to do that.

But now he'd be *here*...

Would that help somehow? she suddenly wondered.

Over and over today she'd tortured herself with the thought that this last week with him was all she was ever going to have. And as difficult as it had been to end her engagement to Trent, accepting that this was the end with Wyatt had been even worse.

Picturing Wyatt moving to Northbridge permanently, becoming a part of her community, did make her consider if, on her own home turf, she couldn't better fight and conquer any compulsion she might have to compete with his late wife. It made her consider if she couldn't—and wouldn't—be more likely to be herself if they built their life in Northbridge.

She hadn't seemed to have a problem with it since they'd met. And she wouldn't be stepping into Wyatt's world—the way she'd stepped into Trent's. Wyatt would be stepping into hers.

Hope sprang to life in her. Hope she wanted to hang on to, because even before she'd left him in her driveway that afternoon she'd realized that she loved him. More deeply than she'd ever loved anyone.

She had to admit that Wyatt had never even hinted at pressuring her to be anyone or anything but herself. Or to reconstruct something that he'd lost. Something he was now willing to put completely behind him.

Could she believe that he truly had grieved for his

wife and baby and the life he'd thought he would have, that he *had* put it behind him? That what he actually *wanted* was her—for herself—and a totally new and different life with her?

Because if she could believe that, then maybe they *did* have a chance…

"Neily? Are you still with me?" he was asking, drawing her out of her own thoughts and back to the moment.

"You're moving here for a fresh start," she said to prove she knew exactly what was going on. Then, recalling what he'd said about not faulting her for not being impulsive, she said, "Was Mikayla impulsive?"

"Not particularly. And nothing about her had anything to do with this morning. The only thing—and I mean the absolute *only* thing—on my mind was that I'm in love with you and I want you to be my wife, that I couldn't stand the idea that I'd bring you home today, go back to Missoula, and that would be it for us. And I'm not going to *let* this be it for us," he added.

"I don't want this to be it for us, either," Neily heard herself say even before she was certain that it would be all right if she did. "Maybe I'm more impulsive than you thought."

He smiled hopefully himself, but he didn't push. And left to sort through this more, she said, "I did a lot of thinking today and I know you haven't done anything to try to turn me into Mikayla—or into anything I'm not. I know you haven't done anything that should have made me believe you were trying to use me to recapture what you lost. That this was about my own issues of living up to either what *is* expected of me or to just what I think might be—"

"So maybe this is just a case of *you* needing to let go of my past," he suggested gently.

That actually had a ring of truth to it and she laughed a small, wry laugh in response. "I guess I have been hanging on to it. Worrying about living up to someone I never even met or knew."

He closed the distance between them then and came to stand in front of her, taking her shoulders in his big hands. "So leave my past alone," he commanded in a tone that enticed, too. "Let us have what we have and forget the rest."

Could she let go of his past? she asked herself. And her own? She knew she was going to have to try. Because the here and now was too sweet, and she wanted him and a future with him too much to turn her back on the opportunity.

"I do love you," she told him, raising a hand to his chest.

His arms went around her so he could pull her against him. "And that—and that I love you," he said firmly, "are the only things that matter."

He kissed her then, and the minute his lips took hers she knew that she would never have been able to go the rest of her life without that. Without him. Especially when that one kiss went from tender to passionate to sexy and was enough to set things off again as if the night before in the hotel room had never ended.

Her hoodie and his T-shirt came off. Jeans and underwear were flung aside to free the way for hands and mouths to explore and reclaim what had been discovered so recently.

The sunroom floor was not a comfortable bed and yet Neily barely noticed as Wyatt laid her down on it and slipped into her as if that was where he was meant to be.

She lost awareness of everything but his amazing body above her, inside of her, as he took them to an all-new height made even greater by the knowledge that this was only a beginning for them.

Then, when each of them was satisfied and satiated, they both collapsed—Wyatt to his back, Neily on her side pressed to his, her head pillowed by the bulging biceps of the arm he had raised alongside that face she knew she would never tire of looking at.

"And *that* is why I knew I had a chance," Wyatt bragged after they'd caught their breath.

"Oh, really…" Neily challenged.

"Nothing that good between any two people can just be left in a retirement village in Sheridan, Wyoming."

Neily laughed. "No, I suppose not."

"So," he said then, rubbing her arm with his free hand. "Can we be the next Northbridge wedding?"

"I think that can be arranged."

"Unless you want a long, drawn-out deal with engagement announcements and parties and showers and—"

"I don't want long and drawn-out," she assured him. All she wanted was him, and she wanted him again right then.

Which she let him know by pressing down with the thigh that was draped over him.

Wyatt let out a sound that was part groan, part growl, brought the arm she was lying on around her and rolled her to lie on top of him, where he was already rising for more.

"I love you, Neily Pratt," he said, looking into her eyes so intently she could see how deeply his feelings ran.

"I love you, too," she whispered because her own emotions flooded her in answer to what she saw in him.

He cupped her head in his hands and pulled her down to kiss him again, an all-consuming kiss that not only awakened renewed yearnings but also seemed to seal their commitment to each other.

And it was then that, in her heart, Neily knew that just as no one in her past could compare to him, he wasn't comparing her to anyone in his. Or expecting her to be anything but what she was. Or wanting anything of her but to share the fresh start that would launch their future.

Because what they'd found together, in each other, was one of a kind.

It was completely their own.

And it was better than anything that had come before it.

* * * * *

Don't miss Marti Grayson's story,
the next chapter in Victoria Pade's miniseries
NORTHBRIDGE NUPTIALS.
Coming soon to Silhouette Special Edition.

*Here's a sneak peek at THE CEO'S CHRISTMAS
PROPOSITION, the first in* USA TODAY *bestselling
author Merline Lovelace's* HOLIDAYS ABROAD
trilogy coming in November 2008.

American Devon McShay is about to get the
Christmas surprise of a lifetime when she meets
her new client, sexy billionaire Caleb Logan, for
the very first time.

Silhouette

Desire

Available November 2008

Her breath whistled out in a sigh of relief when he exited Customs. Devon recognized him right away from the newspaper and magazine articles her friend and partner Sabrina had looked up during her frantic prep work.

Caleb John Logan, Jr. Thirty-one. Six-two. With jet-black hair, laser-blue eyes and a linebacker's shoulders under his charcoal-gray cashmere overcoat. His jaw-dropping good looks didn't score him any points with Devon. She'd learned the hard way not to trust handsome heartbreakers like Cal Logan.

But he was a client. An important one. And she was willing to give someone who'd served a hitch in the marines before earning a B.S. from the University of Oregon, an MBA from Stanford and his first million at the ripe old age of twenty-six the benefit of the doubt.

Right up until he spotted the hot-pink pashmina, that is.

Devon knew the flash of color was more visible than the sign she held up with his name on it. So she wasn't surprised when Logan picked her out of the crowd and cut in her direction. She'd just plastered on her best businesswoman smile when he whipped an arm around her waist. The next moment she was sprawled against his cashmere-covered chest.

"Hello, brown eyes."

Swooping down, he covered her mouth with his.

Sheer astonishment kept Devon rooted to the spot for a few seconds while her mind whirled chaotically. Her first thought was that her client had downed a few too many drinks during the long flight. Her second, that he'd mistaken the kind of escort and consulting services her company provided. Her third shoved everything else out of her head.

The man could kiss!

His mouth moved over hers with a skill that ignited sparks at a half dozen flash points throughout her body. Devon hadn't experienced that kind of spontaneous combustion in a while. A *long* while.

The sparks were still popping when she pushed off his chest, only now they fueled a flush of anger.

"Do you always greet women you don't know with a lip-lock, Mr. Logan?"

A smile crinkled the skin at the corners of his eyes. "As a matter of fact, I don't. That was from Don."

"Huh?"

"He said he owed you one from New Year's Eve two years ago and made me promise to deliver it."

She stared up at him in total incomprehension. Logan hooked a brow and attempted to prompt a non-existent memory.

"He abandoned you at the Waldorf. Five minutes before midnight. To deliver twins."

"I don't have a clue who or what you're…"

Understanding burst like a water balloon.

"Wait a sec. Are you talking about Sabrina's old boyfriend? Your buddy, who's now an ob-gyn doc?"

It was Logan's turn to look startled. He recovered faster than Devon had, though. His smile widened into a rueful grin.

"I take it you're not Sabrina Russo."

"No, Mr. Logan, I am *not*."

* * * * *

Be sure to look for
THE CEO'S CHRISTMAS PROPOSITION
by Merline Lovelace.
Available in November 2008 wherever books are sold, including most bookstores, supermarkets, drugstores and discount stores.

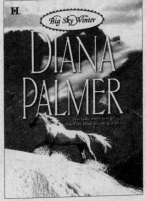

Romantic
SUSPENSE

**Sparked by Danger,
Fueled by Passion.**

Lindsay McKenna
Susan Grant

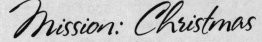

Celebrate the holidays with a pair
of military heroines and their daring men
in two romantic, adventurous stories
from these bestselling authors.

Featuring:

"The Christmas Wild Bunch"
by *USA TODAY* bestselling author
Lindsay McKenna

and

"Snowbound with a Prince"
by *New York Times* bestselling author
Susan Grant

Available November wherever books are sold.

REQUEST YOUR FREE BOOKS!

2 FREE NOVELS PLUS 2 FREE GIFTS!

SPECIAL EDITION®

Life, Love and Family!

YES! Please send me 2 FREE Silhouette Special Edition® novels and my 2 FREE gifts (gifts are worth about $10). After receiving them, if I don't wish to receive any more books, I can return the shipping statement marked "cancel." If I don't cancel, I will receive 6 brand-new novels every month and be billed just $4.24 per book in the U.S. or $4.99 per book in Canada, plus 25¢ shipping and handling per book and applicable taxes, if any*. That's a savings of at least 15% off the cover price! I understand that accepting the 2 free books and gifts places me under no obligation to buy anything. I can always return a shipment and cancel at any time. Even if I never buy another book from Silhouette, the two free books and gifts are mine to keep forever.

235 SDN EEYU 335 SDN EEY6

Name	(PLEASE PRINT)	
Address		Apt. #
City	State/Prov.	Zip/Postal Code

Signature (if under 18, a parent or guardian must sign)

Mail to the **Silhouette Reader Service:**
IN U.S.A.: P.O. Box 1867, Buffalo, NY 14240-1867
IN CANADA: P.O. Box 609, Fort Erie, Ontario L2A 5X3

Not valid to current subscribers of Silhouette Special Edition books.

Want to try two free books from another line?
Call 1-800-873-8635 or visit www.morefreebooks.com.

* Terms and prices subject to change without notice. N.Y. residents add applicable sales tax. Canadian residents will be charged applicable provincial taxes and GST. Offer not valid in Quebec. This offer is limited to one order per household. All orders subject to approval. Credit or debit balances in a customer's account(s) may be offset by any other outstanding balance owed by or to the customer. Please allow 4 to 6 weeks for delivery. Offer available while quantities last.

Your Privacy: Silhouette is committed to protecting your privacy. Our Privacy Policy is available online at www.eHarlequin.com or upon request from the Reader Service. From time to time we make our lists of customers available to reputable third parties who may have a product or service of interest to you. If you would prefer we not share your name and address, please check here. ☐

SSE08R

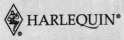

HARLEQUIN®

American ★ Romance®

LAURA MARIE ALTOM
A Daddy
for Christmas

THE STATE OF PARENTHOOD

Single mom Jesse Cummings is struggling
to run her Oklahoma ranch and raise her
two little girls after the death of her husband.
Then on Christmas Eve, a miracle strolls onto
her land in the form of tall, handsome bull
rider Gage Moore. He doesn't plan on staying,
but in the season of miracles, anything
can happen....

**Available November
wherever books are sold.**

LOVE, HOME & HAPPINESS

www.eHarlequin.com   HAR75237

COMING NEXT MONTH

SSECNM1008BPA